# BLOOD
## *Sistas*

**The Chronicals of Black Uptown Girlz
Growing up in the Hood**

# Munesta Faulkner

**Outskirts Press, Inc.**
**Denver, Colorado**

Blood Sistas
The Chronicals of Black Uptown Girlz Growing Up in the Hood
All Rights Reserved.
Copyright © 2009 Munesta Faulkner
v3.0 r1.0

Destine Rogers, Ebony Belcher, Alexis L. Walker and Shaniqua Pugh. The front cover, back cover and logo was designed by Mike Owens for Mike O Photography

Outskirts Press, Inc.
http://www.outskirtspress.com

ISBN: 978-0-578-01610-8

PRINTED IN THE UNITED STATES OF AMERICA

# Acknowledgements

I would like to offer a special thank-you to my manager,
Elaine Owens, for her unwavering support.

I also wish to thank the following individuals:
Monique Tatum, Renee Evans,
Superior and Yvonne from Most Hated Entertainment,
Romello "Moe" Cooper, Kym, Donny Gripper, Robert Laprae,
Floyd Cromwell, Dr. Jim Bostic, James Hackett, Mrs. Jackson,
Jason from ACA, Ronald Miller, Tasha Jones, and
Anthony Matthews from Final Touch.

# Introduction of a Blood Sista

This is a story about my crazy life. Over the years, a lot of things have happened to make me a much stronger person. I have learned a great deal about friendship.

This is my life with my girls—my crew—Sabrina, Rochelle and Dominique. We met in second grade in New York City. Sabrina lived on Amsterdam Avenue and 151st Street. Rochelle lived in the Polo Grounds on 155th. Dominique lived on 145th and Broadway, and me, I lived on 148th Street and Broadway. The way that we acted back then, we still act like that to this day.

Even though we were very different, it seemed like our lives were meant to intertwine and overlap. But no matter what, I knew that I would never find three best friends like them, again, in life. This is my story about four best friends growing up in the hood.

## CHAPTER ONE

# Four Friends with Big Dreams

First, there is me, Gabrielle Ritchie. I have a pretty big family, five brothers and no sisters. That alone has made me tough over the years, especially after all the beatings that I endured at the hands of my middle brother Marcus Anthony. We call him Boy. My grandmother, Tracy, used to call him that and it just kind of stuck.

My grandmother passed away from pancreatic cancer. For years the doctors would say that they didn't have the slightest idea what was wrong with her. All we knew was that she just kept getting sick and going in and out of the hospital. My grandmother was a big woman and a few years before she died, she mysteriously lost a lot of weight. That sent up red flags to the whole family, because she's from the South, and we love to eat.

Her death really took a toll on Marcus because they were extremely close. He lived with her on and off for many years. No matter what he was doing, he would always go to my grandmother's house to check and see if she needed anything. Even if he had to walk there in a blizzard, he would go just to make sure that she was okay.

She was a very strong woman to be a single parent, raising seven kids on her own. She acted as though she gave birth to Marcus too. She gave him money, bought him clothes, and basically gave him whatever he wanted. You can say that out of all of us, Boy was obviously her favorite. Plus, she was very overprotective with him. And what would really irk my nerves is that he could never do any wrong in her eyes. He was right even when he was wrong.

His love was so strong for her that he preferred spending time with her over time with his friends. They were the best of friends. She obviously gave him the love and affection that he felt he wasn't getting from our parents due to their working all the time. Sadly, when she died, he fell into a state of depression. After that he didn't want to be bothered by anyone.

He became a loner, and chose not to have any friends. My parents tried desperately to get him to talk to someone, but he adamantly refused. He just stayed locked up in his room watching cartoons all day, for days on end. My parents felt that we should give him some time to grieve, so they left him alone. They gave him time to grieve all right. And that gave him more than enough time on his hands to fuck with me, to make my life a living hell. He had a lot of anger inside pertaining to my grandmother's death. He refused to let any of the family get close enough to try and help him.

He started out slowly, just hitting me for no reason, claiming that he wanted me to be prepared for life and to make sure that no one would ever take advantage of me…so he constantly fought me. Back then I was a scrawny little kid, and I was scared of my own shadow. I wasn't a confrontational person, so everyone punked me all the time.

Marcus wasn't having that. He used to say, "No sister of mine is going to be weak."

Every time I turned around, this asshole was fighting or hitting me. I couldn't understand for the life of me why he would want to fight his own sister. I asked him repeatedly why he kept doing it. And his lame excuse was always that he was just looking out for my best interests.

*Now do I look stupid to you?* I never once believed that. It was just his sick twisted rationale for wanting to fight me. I guess that it made him sleep better at night, knowing that he could pound on his younger sibling and get away with it. It was like a game to him. Pretty much, there were no repercussions, because he always did it when nobody was around. So no one believed me. They felt that I was just telling stories and crying wolf.

I believe that my parents felt guilty because they worked all the time, which basically left us raising ourselves. They always left Marcus in charge of me since he was four years older.

My parents felt bad that he was depressed about my grandmother's death, so they basically kissed his ass. That was unlucky for me. Marcus was never concerned about my being tough. He just wanted to use me as a punching bag. As a result of all that abuse, I became tough inside and out. I became slick with the mouth and fly with the hands as my confidence level grew.

I fought like a Brooklyn girl once Marcus got finished with me. He trained me like I was a heavyweight boxer getting ready for a big payday. I used to hate it because he had me lifting weights and running two miles every single morning. Even though I was reluctant and stubborn, in the end it paid off with a banging little physique. From first glance, you would totally underestimate me, but you would surely be in for a surprise if you chose to step to me.

My nickname is Gabby because as you can tell, I love to talk. I have spent hours on the phone talking to my friends. I never had a problem making friends because of my bubbly personality. People are drawn to me right away. And that's what attracted Rochelle, Sabrina and Dominique to accept me as their friend.

I knew from the time I was a child that whatever path or career I chose, I was destined to succeed.

## Sabrina

Next, I need to introduce Sabrina Daniels. She has five brothers and five sisters. She's a selfish, self-centered person. She's cheap when it comes to others and doesn't have a problem spending your money. Sabrina wants the finer things in life and feels those can be obtained by force, persistence or any means necessary, if that's what it takes. Since her family barely scraped by, she was forced to wear the hand-me-downs of her older sister Monique. She hated that and said it made her feel like a bum. The girls in our school could have laughed and talked about her, but they knew better and kept it to themselves.

Sabina often said that when she got older, she would make a better life for herself and have the best of everything. That was going to happen no matter what the cost or who she had to hurt to get it. Some of her men were just casualties, and they should have known better than to fall in love with her.

She constantly talked about having a fancy car, a good job and a nice house. Since Sabrina was looking to be a kept woman, she would figure out who she had to manipulate to make that happen. Some people would call that a gold digger, but she called it love. Sabrina is a very smart, outgoing people person. One of the things that irritated me was that she had to be in control at all times.

Everyone always loved Sabrina. As a result she became the

leader of our clique. She couldn't stand to be ignored. You know what else was sickening? When she talked, Rochelle and Dominique busted their asses to listen, like she was God. And they catered to her even if she was wrong.

## Rochelle

Next in line is Rochelle Benson. Out of the four of us, she is the vainest. She didn't want to be bothered with you unless you benefitted her or you were up to her standards. She's very judgmental when it comes to friendships. She was extremely picky about who she chose to be her friend. But, if you got the chance to get to know her, you were lucky. She's a good person with a good heart. She would do anything for you if she liked you. A lot of people mistakenly rubbed her the wrong way, so they caught the bitchy side of her. She's a Gemini, so you never really knew who you were dealing with from day to day.

I used to wonder if she took medication to calm herself down with that split personality that she had going on. One thing that I hated about her is that Rochelle had a bad habit of holding a grudge. If you did something to her, you better watch out, because you might not like what the outcome would be. She could be very explosive. Plus, she would never let you forget what you'd done to her.

She always said that she would forgive but would never forget. And the craziest thing with her was, if she did anything to you, she would expect to be forgiven immediately. Ain't that a bitch.

I always felt bad for her though, because at the age of six, Rochelle was placed in a foster home due to her mother's neglect. Her mother constantly had different men in and out of the house after her dead-beat dad left. And her mother's scum bag boyfriend, Ray, tried to molest Rochelle repeatedly. What hurt Rochelle the most was that her mother wouldn't even believe her own daughter. She would rather believe Ray because she didn't want to be lonely. Even though he treated her like shit. What a low-life. Her mother was a beautiful woman and could have done much better.

A six-year-old girl shouldn't have to go through that. After her mother confronted Ray with Rochelle's allegations, he couldn't stand the sight of the little girl anymore. He started telling lies on Rochelle and treating her badly when her mother wasn't around. And to add insult to injury, he constantly talked in her mother's ear about how disrespectful Rochelle was being. What the hell did he expect? She got to her breaking point and finally got the courage to speak on it.

Then, he finally convinced her mother to place her in a foster home. Ain't that a kick in the ass. Rochelle felt so betrayed, and from that point on, it became increasingly hard for her to trust. And when she did and you betrayed her, she took it very hard. When we met, my mother and father took a liking to her right away, especially after learning about everything that she had already been through. So Rochelle quickly became part of our family.

Her foster parents, Mr. and Mrs. Poole, they were cool and understood the need for Rochelle to be comfortable. They really had her best interests at heart, and they wanted her to be happy. And if she was happy staying at my house, they definitely didn't have a problem with that. She looked expensive and very well put together, even if her clothes and shoes came from the discount stores, like Walton's. To others, Rochelle appeared to be unapproachable, and that's the way she liked it.

Another thing that upset me about Rochelle is that she had a bad temper that she sometimes couldn't control. Once you made her mad, it was very hard to calm her down. I even made the mistake of getting her mad by touching her brush, and she stayed mad at me for well over two weeks.

No matter what, Sabrina knew what to say to either calm Rochelle down or push her buttons. Thank God for Sabrina. She was finally able to convince her just how petty she was acting.

Rochelle is not a troublemaker, but if you cross her, she doesn't have a problem fighting you. She is very direct and she tells you exactly what is on her mind. Rest assured, after that, you can take it any way you want. Trust me. It didn't even matter to her, as long as she got to speak her mind.

A lot of girls growing up wanted to fight her, just because she is beautiful and she knows it. All the boys, as long as I could remember, wanted to date her, so she was never without a boy-friend for long, unless she wanted to be. And for that reason, the girls were jealous of her and tried to steal her boyfriends, but none of those skeezers could ever accomplish that.

## Dominique

Lastly, there is Dominique Johnson, but we all call her Diamond. She got that nickname because she likes to shine and always loves to be the center of attention. She is an only child, so we became her family. When Dominique and I met, we clicked right away. We were the closest, out of all four of us. I could talk to her about anything or anyone and never have to worry about it being repeated.

Diamond is into fashion, and her love for clothes made her want to design stylish clothing for all. Since her family didn't have much money, she was forced to improvise. She always had a new way to wear her clothes to make you think that they were new or that she spent a lot on them. Everyone would ask her where she shopped and got her clothes, not knowing that she designed them herself. She always dreamed as a child of how she wanted to start an affordable clothing line for average consumers who didn't have a lot of money to spend on their gear. Sometimes we would dress alike to show off her ideas, and people would see that they were original. We made a promise to one another to make that dream of a clothing line become a reality. We even came up with the name "Unique Expressions." That name came about because of me, since I had a hard time expressing myself. Diamond always encouraged me and told me not to worry about anything, because whatever the problem, there is a solution. And most of all, to just pray on it and everything will be okay.

Let me explain something to you. I love Rochelle and Sabrina to death, but they have certain ways about them that irritate me and get on my fucking nerves. Sometimes they act stuck up and constantly talk about themselves, but I still love them dearly. They are my dogs. The thing that I cherished about our friendship is that we could express ourselves to one another, get mad, fight, yell, or scream at each other. We would get over it and could never stay angry for too long. Besides, Sabrina is the peacemaker and she would always find a way to get us talking again.

Oddly enough, Sabrina was so gifted that you could see her committing a crime, and she would deny it and tell you that it was her twin. Even though you knew better, you would still believe her because she has the gift of gab and appears to be innocent.

Hell, we are family, so that's how it's supposed to be. Like the Corleones in the *The Godfather* movie, the number one rule is you never go against the family. No matter what, your family will have your back whether you are right or wrong. If there is a beef taking place, we handle it and ask questions later. If a betrayal of any sort takes place, or there's a weak link, you have to get rid of them for dishonoring the family. We don't like embarrassment, so it's just easier to make the problem, or you, disappear.

## CHAPTER TWO

# The Beginning

## THE OOZING OUT OF THE BLOOD

When we were younger, we were inseparable. We were like the four musketeers—Sabrina, Rochelle, Dominique, and me, Gabrielle. We met in the second grade in Mrs. Thompson's class. We were only eight years old at the time. That's a long time to be friends. Most friendships don't even last half that long. I can't believe that we've been friends for over twenty years. We did some crazy things back then. I think that individually we were missing something in our lives, and we just wanted to belong and to be a part of something.

Sabrina came up with the idea of becoming blood sisters, since we were so close and we acted that way anyway. She said that we should cut each other on the finger and drink each other's blood. Then, officially, we would be blood sisters for life. We made a pact that we were going to be family until the day that we died.

Now I guess that it's safe to say, we will always have each other's back. No one could ever infiltrate the love that we have for each other.

Subsequently, for my sisters, I would do anything without even giving a second thought. As we grew into adulthood, the bond between us four was unbreakable. Everyone on the block already knew that if you mess with one, get ready for a beat down. We might look like we can't fight, but we gets it in.

Our daily routine, outside of our jobs, consisted of talking on the phone to each other three or four times a day. We always communicated to each other what was going on in our lives, so there was nothing that you could tell me bad or otherwise about them.

We looked so fly whenever went to the club. No matter how many women were there, we always got all the attention. Since Diamond loves to dance and choreograph, she would teach us the latest dances while adding her own style. We got the dances in no time, since we are fast learners. When we would get on the dance floor, people would try to emulate our well-rehearsed dance moves. We had a fly name for ourselves, The Uptown Girls, since we resided uptown.

Our clique was exclusive, so we even sported jackets with the name of our crew. That was Sabrina's idea. She felt like the bitches out there could not touch us. A lot of girls were jealous of us but still wanted to be down. Well, that was never going to happen, because we were the bomb. Our team was very selective, so we rarely let outside people into our inner circle. We would have to vote on it, but Sabrina had the final say. Usually she was always right; therefore, we rarely went against her judgment.

Since Thursday was ladies night, we decided to all go to Club Rumba, on Columbus Circle and 59th Street. We went there every week because they have two-for-one drink specials before 10:00 p.m. We met up after work, so we could unwind after a long, draining day.

On this particular night, this guy named Jared Jeffries spotted us in the club. He was admiring us while we were dancing. When we were done, he walked over to Sabrina and handed her a business card.

Then he said with a smile, "Hi, I'm Jared Jeffries, and I'm from Reck House Management. I manage an up-and-coming rapper called Tek 1, and he needs dancers for his video called 'A Gangster's Wish.' You've heard of him right?"

Sabrina smiled and said, "Yeah, I think I heard of him on a couple of mixed tapes from DJ Eddie F. He used to be with the group Heavy D and the Boys."

"Well," Jared replied, "the way you guys were moving on the floor just now, I know that he will love you. Your style is captivating. I haven't seen anything like that. By the way, who came up with those moves?"

Diamond smiled. "It's just a little something I put together."

"You ladies really complement each other and that's really hard to find," he said. "Tek 1 needs good dancers to help him, because he's not a good dancer, but lyrically he's dope. Nobody can see him. Plus, I know that all the men in the audience will be turned on by your uniqueness and the beauty each one of you possesses."

I thought, Ding! ding! ding! Good answer. He didn't have to convince me anymore, because I was already sold. Nevertheless, he told us to think about it and then give him a call. And if we were interested, then he would set up an audition for Tek 1.

We were so excited, but we didn't want to seem too thirsty. After he walked off and faded into the crowd, we screamed with excitement at the top of our lungs. We waited a few weeks, and then Sabrina called Jared to set up the audition. Dominique needed time to come up with a routine. She let her creative mind go and got on her grind. After about forty-eight hours, she came up with a dope routine. Two weeks later, we auditioned for Tek 1, and we blew him away. He quickly snatched us up and told us to put something together for his video.

Why wouldn't we do it? It was a great opportunity, and we would get a lot of exposure doing what we loved, while getting paid for it. What more could you ask for? We shot the video on four separate days. It took really long hours and was quite tiring, but it was worth it in the end.

Tek 1 was very impressed with the response from all of the video shows, like *Video Music Box*, and the shows on BET and VH-1. Now he wanted us to dance for him on his upcoming world tour. We were ecstatic, like kids in a candy store.

We obtained an entertainment lawyer, Cameron Russell, to look over the contract. He told us that everything was okay and to sign it. We went all over the world, traveling to places that we had never been before. We worked in countries like Germany, France, China and the U.K., just to name a few. We were on tour for about a year and a half, on and off. Momma never said that there would be days like this. As dancers we really didn't make much money, but we had more than enough.

## CHAPTER THREE

# Things Don't Always Appear as They Seem

It was really nerve-racking dealing with Sabrina at one point because she was under a lot of stress. She was constantly fighting with her then-boyfriend Philip. The funny part about that was that I met Philip first. He was my friend. He always liked me as more than just a friend, but I never thought of him that way. He's just fun to be around, and he always makes me laugh.

Philip is very protective over me and that scares me. He really didn't want me to have other male friends, especially if he knew that they were feeling me too. Philip was looking for a relationship and I wasn't. I had just gotten out of a relationship with my ex-boyfriend Thomas, who was a stalker, and I didn't have time for that.

Since Sabrina was always talking about how sexy and cute Philip was, I was tempted to hook them up. Then he could leave me the hell alone. Both of them were getting on my last nerve. Sabrina was constantly begging me to hook them up and put in a good word for her. I constantly told her I didn't think that it would be a good idea, being that I knew his feelings toward me.

Sabrina had a deaf ear when it comes to hearing anything negative about Philip. She felt like he was playing hard to get, because sometimes he would flirt with her. When he started doing that, Sabrina was open. Take that time when we were hanging out and drinking. He was acting like they were a couple, holding her hand and kissing her. I know for sure that I didn't want to have a problem between Sabrina and me. I could feel it and see it coming. Sabrina assured me that it wasn't and started getting an attitude with me. She felt like, if he was just a friend, then I shouldn't have a problem hooking them up, unless I was lying to her about the way that I truly felt toward him. I just said "fuck it," and against my better judgment, I made it happen for them, and they finally made the connection.

When I brought it up to Philip at first, he didn't want to hear it. He said, "Gabby, why do you ask me to do that knowing that I'm still madly in love with you? I would just be fucking with her head because I can. And I know that I'm going to take advantage of her. And if I can get some free ass every now and then, that's what's up."

I kept telling him that nothing is ever going to happen between him and me, ever. Finally, after I am constantly reiterating this to him, then and only then, did he decide to give her a chance. They went strong for about a year, and shortly after that, things started going downhill really fast. That's when there were constant arguments between them and the problems started getting worse. Since I was friends with both of them, I tried to stay neutral. Believe me it was very hard. And it became draining because, at separate times, they would both come to me for advice. It made me feel very uncomfortable and it kept me in the middle.

It was more so Philip, because he would always let it be known to everyone around us that he still carried feelings for me. Whenever I was around, no matter where it was, he would constantly flirt with me. There were many times that this man came on to me after they were together. I remember one instance very clearly. It was a Friday night and we were going to meet up with our boyfriends at VIP, a barbershop where Philip worked. He was a manager there.

The place was nice. It had eight chairs, and at each of the stations in the wall, there was a nineteen-inch flat screen television. That was a good idea, because it was more enticing for the customers, and they could watch movies, cable or sports while they were getting their hair cut. My boyfriend's name was Eugene, but they call him Gene for short. Rochelle's boyfriend was Tyree, but they call him Ty for short. They are co-owners of the barbershop and also best friends who worked hard and saved their money. They hustled if you know what I mean. They are very smart businessmen. They knew enough to get in and get out, because the streets were watching.

Their silent partner is Devon Jenkins. That was Dominique's man. He's Ty's cousin. He's a designer who graduated from FIT, The Fashion Institute of Technology. He graduated at the top of his class. His designs were new and inventive.

They all invested their money in a clothing line and called it "Sabastian Valentino," urban clothing for the streets. It caught on like wildfire, and all the kids around the way were wearing it. And before you knew it, people came from all over just to buy their clothes.

The barbershop was always busy, because they treated you like family. Most of the time, the regulars would come there and stay for hours just kicking it. The shop had a good following and was always able to attract new customers through word of mouth. It got to the point where you would have to make an appointment in advance, or you would wind up waiting for hours, especially if there was a boxing match or a championship game on.

At Christmas, we would throw a little party in there. They would give some kids from around the way gifts when the parents couldn't afford to. That was their way of giving back to the community for supporting them, because without the loyal customers, their barbershop wouldn't be as successful. I loved that about them. Even on New Year's Eve, before we went out, we would always have the first drink there right before midnight to bring in the new year. Like us, our boyfriends were very tight and they all hung out together.

I especially liked the fact they had these comfortable leather couches in the shop. Many a night I would wind up falling asleep on them while I was waiting for Gene to finish. In the middle of the floor, they always kept a chilled bottle of Absolute Vodka, Hypnotiq or Hennessy on hand. Usually at night after closing time, our boyfriends would sit around and parley. They would pop a bottle of choice while talking about things like sports, news, who was the best rapper of all times, and the most important thing in their lives…us, the Girls. At least once a week we would go chill with them after closing time. Shit, that was okay with me, because as long as they had a bottle of Henny, I was good.

## CHAPTER FOUR

# Oops You Fell for It

### HOOK, LINE AND SINKER

One particular night, we pulled up in front of the barbershop in Rochelle's Jeep. I was not feeling good; I think that I had a stomach virus. I couldn't seem to hold anything down that day. Plus, I had a lot of things on my mind. After we got inside and showed our boyfriends some love, then I decided to go outside and smoke a cigarette. Gene was cutting someone's hair, and he had two or three people waiting patiently. Seconds later, Sabrina and Dominique came outside.

"Gabby, what's wrong?" Sabrina asked. "You really look stressed. You didn't have too much to say the whole way over here."

"Yeah girl," Dominique said, "you know if you're going through something, we are always here for you."

Then she walked over and gave me a hug. And you know that really made me feel a whole lot better. I guess that's what I really needed.

"We're going to the Jamaican restaurant to get something to eat," Sabrina said. "Do you want something?"

"No, not for me, I'm not really hungry," I said. "Wait. Pick up a small oxtail dinner with rice and peas for Gene."

I gave her a ten dollar bill. Sabrina took it and said, "Okay, we will be back in a few."

Then they jumped in the Jeep and pulled off with the music blasting a Jay Z song called "A Hard Knock Life." I turned around and looked through the glass and saw that Rochelle was nowhere in sight. She must have been in the back with her boyfriend Ty. Rochelle is a freak, so who knew what they were doing back there. I turned back around and kept puffing on my cigarette. Then a strange feeling came over me. It felt like someone was staring at me from behind. I heard the door open, but I paid it no mind.

As I looked to my left, I noticed Philip standing there. He was staring at me all googley eyed with a big smile on his face. I asked him what was wrong.

"Oh nothing, I'm good now," he replied nonchalantly. "You know if I was your man…"

Before he could utter another word, I looked at him and rolled my eyes. Then I sighed, because I knew that I was in for it.

I asked, "Didn't we go over this time and time again?"

He acted like he didn't even hear a thing that I said. "I'm so jealous of Gene," he responded. "He's got a very good-looking woman. My God, you're so beautiful." Then he started licking his lips while shaking his head.

He looked me up and down and continued, "When are you going to give me those jewels? Boy, I would love for you to be my baby momma. You would be well taken care of, and you wouldn't have to want for anything. You would be my ebony princess."

Then he grabbed his penis and adjusted it because he had a really big bulge in his pants. He was making me feel very uncomfortable. And I started feeling sick.

"Listen Philip, you're going to stop disrespecting me like that.

You know that I'm in a relationship with Gene, so you know that's never going to happen. Even if I wasn't in a relationship, I still wouldn't sleep with you. I'm in love with my man. He's very good to me. Besides aren't you with Sabrina? The energy that you're putting into me, you should be putting into your relationship with her."

As usual, he would just ignore what I said when it came to her.

Then he said, "You already know what it is between her and me. I wish that you would get that through your head. I'm only with her because you asked me to; that's how much I love you."

I just shook my head. It's pointless to finish this conversation with him, I thought. I'm so frustrated with this knucklehead, so I'll just finish my cigarette and go back inside. This fool is giving me a massive headache. I'm at my wit's end with this shit, and I can't take it anymore.

Once inside, I walked over to Gene and give him a very passionate kiss on the lips. Then I walked over to the couch and sat my ass down. A few minutes later, Philip came back inside with a smirk on his face. He looked at me and winked while he was walking past me. He walked over to the cash register and sat down behind the counter, still staring at me. I ignored him and continued watching *The Jeffersons* on TV Land. About ten minutes later, Sabrina and Diamond pulled up in the Jeep, and Philip quickly jumped up and ran outside to help them with the bags. He gave Sabrina a kiss on the lips, as he was staring at me while they walked inside.

Dealing with him is like watching a soap opera or a very successful reality show. He's got so much game. He's so believable, he should get into acting. Because then he had the nerve to say to her, "Baby I missed you. What took you so long? You know how

I get when you are out of my sight for a long period of time."

He smiled at me while saying that to her. I laughed. Yeah, I thought, I know how you are when she's not around. Not ten minutes ago, you were trying to get in my drawers.

I shook my head and rolled my eyes in disgust. I wished that I had minded my business and never gotten them together. Plain and simple, he's a dog. He's a trip because whenever he confides in me about their up and down relationship, he honestly thinks that I'm going take his side. Mistakenly, in his own twisted mind, he still thinks that we will wind up together. I still have regrets where he's concerned, but not enough to make the same mistake twice.

I had to hit him in the head and bust his bubble again because it was becoming an everyday thing, and he was getting on my nerves. Even that day at the barbershop after flirting with me all that time, as soon as Sabrina came back, he acted like he never said anything out of the way to me.

This went on for longer than I liked. It got so bad that even Rochelle and Dominique started asking me, "What's up with that?" The more that I told them nothing, the more they acted like they didn't believe me. Rochelle was constantly telling me that I was wrong for not telling Sabrina and leading Philip on… *Can you believe that?* Huh, me leading him on.

If they had only known what I was going through with this arrogant man. If I had just stopped talking to him out of no-where, Sabrina would have asked questions, and I didn't feel like explaining everything to her. It was pointless to even say any-thing to her. Besides Sabrina was so in love with him that she would never have believed me. He had her shook. She would do anything for him and believe whatever he said. I know several instances where he flat out lied to her, even after she caught him with another woman.

What annoyed me was that they would even believe I could do something like that, especially to my sister. I would never do something as fucked up as that and still be able to be around her every day.

That takes a cold-hearted, calculating person to pull that off. That's not me, and I do have a conscience. When you do things like that, you are asking for whatever your hand calls for, and I take my friendships very seriously.

## CHAPTER FIVE

# Baby Momma Drama

Unexpectedly, Sabrina started throwing up and sleeping a lot. Every chance that she got, she would be sleeping before and after a show. That was very strange, because she was always full of energy and ready for a party. My suspicions were confirmed finally, three months later, after performing on "The Black Out Tour," with Run-DMC, Public Enemy, Ashanti, Alicia Keys, Keyshia Cole, Missy Elliott, Naughty by Nature, and Salt and Pepper. She came into the dressing room holding her stomach. It was over when she lifted her shirt and I could see a little bulge.

Sabrina walked over to where we were sitting. "What's up guys? I have something very important to tell you."

"What's up momma?" Rochelle asked. "What do want to tell us?"

Sabrina paused. "Guess what? I'm pregnant and I don't know what to do."

I just froze with my mouth open, because I couldn't say a word. Even though I had kind of already figured that out, it still took me by surprise.

I was hoping that she had sense enough to run to the clinic and get an abortion, especially the way their relationship was going. Also, let's face it; she really didn't need to deal with a pregnancy at that time.

I know it's awful to say something like that, but again I was just being selfish. I knew that if she did decide to keep the baby, her career would be over. I already knew that we weren't going to replace her, and it wasn't going to be the same without her. After that, she was very indecisive on whether or not to keep the baby.

Since Sabrina was stressed out all the time and constantly spotting on and off, she wound up having a miscarriage. She took it very hard. One minute Philip was happy about having the baby, and the next minute he was treating her fucked up and cursing her out. It was pathetic that she was constantly crying over his stupid ass.

After a trauma like that, Sabrina understandably became depressed and her whole attitude and demeanor changed. Once we finally came off of that grueling tour, she was distant and hard to reach. Our friendship was deteriorating right before my eyes. For the first time in years, I barely saw or talked to her. It seemed like the only person that she was giving rhythm to was Rochelle. Regrettably, when I did get a chance to talk to her on the phone, she would cut me short and talk no longer than five minutes. That felt strange to me, because growing up we would talk on the phone for hours on end.

Now that I look back at it, this whole crazy situation came about because of the feelings that Philip had for me. Every time I turned him down, he would take out his frustrations on her. Even before the miscarriage, things were never really right between them anyway.

I don't know what happened. Philip and I used to be mad cool. So this shit got to me. Just imagine if I did give him some, I would never have been able to get rid of him. He would be like herpes; he would be in love with me for life. There would be no curing him because I would be in his veins, in his heart, and always on his mind. I'd be like crack, just one tote and he'd be hooked.

I was relieved for a second, because out of the blue, he stopped pushing up on me. I thought that I was in the clear, but I guess that I was wrong. The next time we chilled together, he started that shit up again. And as usual, he blamed it on the alcohol.

Personally, I thought as he tried to act out his desires with me that way, due to his drinking, he felt his actions would be excused. You know what? I was tired of making excuses for him. Shit, he was a grown-ass man. Besides, he wasn't my boyfriend, just my friend. If he was really my friend, then he would respect me and know to fall the hell back. And he would already know his actions made it very uncomfortable for us to chill together. But he really didn't give a shit. All he knew was that he wanted it all, having his cake and eating it too. He wanted me to be wifey. And as usual, he was just being selfish. On second thought, I can't blame him.

Anyway, who in his or her right mind, man or woman, could really resist this? Shit, it's not my fault that I'm beautiful…maybe in a different lifetime, or if he wasn't too thirsty, I would have given him some.

I mean, I love the chase, but I know me. If it's too damn easy, then I will walk over him. And it's not worth the risk of losing a good friend. Wait a minute. *Can I be perfectly honest with you guys for a minute?* I've been holding in a series of events that took place well before Sabrina and Philip got together and, of course, before Gene and I ever got together. Now that I look back, I have to admit that what happened was really dumb.

One night Philip and I were chilling at his crib, watching movies, smoking weed, and drinking. For some reason that night I was very horny. I don't know if it was a mixture of the weed and the Henny, but whatever it was, he was looking good to me. Actually he looked damn good. The cologne he was wearing was my favorite, Sean John. The closer he got, the more I got turned on. He sat next to me on the couch wearing a gray crisp wife-beater and a pair of Sean John blue jeans. Maybe he spiked my drink or something, because this was the first time that he ever looked that good to me. I just couldn't control myself. I was thinking crazy sexual thoughts, and I shouldn't have been thinking about him like that, ever!

The rap group, Whodini, said it best, "the freaks come out at night." I guess the freak in me came out that night, and I finally came to terms with it. I started touching his masculine arms while fantasizing what they would feel like while he was holding me. I was longing to kiss him from the moment I saw him. It was more enticing because we were sitting on his European imported couch. I know that he must have gotten much ass on that couch, because as soon as you sat down, you felt like you were in heaven. I know that I could have literally fallen asleep on it, night after night, and become a couch potato.

The way this scene played out, it was like something out of a good urban book. After a couple of drinks I was on fire. I had to feel those juicy lips. The girlz always talk about those suckable lips, so that night I had to test them out for myself. So I pulled him close to me, and we just started making out. One thing led to another and things got sooo hot! My nipples were hard and my body felt hot like a microwave. Philip touched me with his soft, but manly, hands. Then he slid his tongue in my mouth, and we started swapping spit. He made love to my mouth with his tasty tongue. Wow! He was the best kisser that I had experienced in my young, twenty-eight years. While doing that, he caressed my breast and my vagina started gushing with secretions.

Shit! My vagina is so wet right now, I thought, and feels like a waterfall. Niagara Falls to be exact.

I started breathing hard as his soft hands felt my entire body. Our tongues intertwined and ran circles around each other.

Then he stuck his warm hands down my pants and gently massaged my pussy. He's obviously a pro at what he does. Philip eased his fingers inside my pussy, slipping and sliding from all my secretions. His hands must have a built-in GPS, because he knew exactly where to go in a matter of seconds. Philip took control of my clit, and it stood at attention as he gently massaged it with his fingers. With his other hand he slowly unbuttoned my pants. He got up slightly and pushed me back on the couch, putting his muscular body on mine. He touched my stomach like he's a masseur giving a massage. My clit constantly kept twitching, yearning for him to touch it. That was the best feeling ever. He slid his fingers in and out of me like a vibrating dildo. My God. I started screaming at the top of my lungs because it felt so good. He didn't realize what he was doing to me. For once in my life, I wasn't in control, and you know what, I didn't even care. I was just going with the flow, until I couldn't take it anymore and then, I just exploded. It felt like I was cumming through every orifice of my body.

"Oh, my God! Don't stop! Don't stop!"

It felt so good I started speaking in tongues. I didn't know what was going on. I never thought that my pussy could get any wetter than it already was. It was so hard and I couldn't hold back. I was just cumming and cumming. I wanted to achieve that ultimate orgasm again and again. *He better be ready for what he's going to encounter.*

Next, he slowly unbuttoned my shirt, kissing my neck and sucking on it. Ooh…We…He must have found the spot. Then he took his tongue and slowly licked every nook and cranny of my body, starting with my voluptuous breast and then slowly going down my stomach, until he reached my belly button. He slid his tongue in and out my belly button. He slid my panties down and kissed my inner thighs.

Now I couldn't move a muscle. All that was going through my mind was how good he'd feel inside of me. He made his way back up to my lips. I ripped off his shirt and felt his muscular chest. I started kissing on him while unzipping his pants and pulling them down. There in his boxers was a big bulge sticking out, way too much for me to grab. I was so scared to touch it, but I wanted it to go in my mouth.

*I guess I'll try that kinky shit like I practiced on my dildo I call Pinky.* On second thought, this is way too much for me to handle by sticking it in my mouth. So, maybe it's easier for me to ride it and let him try to break down my walls.

I closed my eyes and decided to feel what he was working with. Before I could do that, it fell through his boxers and, wow, it almost blinded me. It was thick, long, and hard as a rock. It was twelve inches of steel that was ready for action. He held it in his hands and then rubbed it against my vagina. That felt so good.

I yelled, "Fuck it…just put it inside."

He looked at me with those sexy, light green eyes, and touched my lips with his fingers and said, "Wait, I have a surprise for you."

Then he made his way down to my vagina. Once down there, Philip wrapped his tongue on my clit and danced around and around. It blew my mind. My mind went blank. I saw stars, while picturing walking on the moon. No gravity, just light and free as a bird. I aggressively grabbed the back of his head and pushed it deeper inside my vagina. I really didn't need to do that because his tongue is extra long, and it felt so good. He nibbled, sucked and stroked it up and down, nice and slow. It was almost as if he was playing a game of tag. Just as I'm getting into it, he suddenly stopped, and my body shivered.

He waited for a few seconds and then continued, and I yelled, "I'm in heaven!"

I wished I could have kept that feeling forever. I wanted to bottle up his tongue and keep it on my nightstand, for when I was hot and horny. Basically, I'm a freak so that's practically every single night. Instead of a vibrator, it would be called a tonguevator. It would be in the shape of his tongue.

It was as if his tongue and my clit were married. They had really good chemistry. Everything was flowing so well and I didn't want it to end! I start screaming his name at the top of my lungs.

"Philip! Philip!" Damn! I know that the whole neighborhood heard me, and I didn't even give a fuck. Shit, all I knew was, he was handling his business. He stayed down there for fifteen to twenty minutes.

I kept thinking about how much I wanted to feel him inside me. I was aggravated because when I pushed his head up to my stomach, he wouldn't budge. He kept giving me resistance. He held his ground, so I just said "fuck it."

I can't stop this orgasm from coming. Like a pregnant woman about to push out her newborn child, it is coming out. It's that time and I'm about to release...there it...goes... flowing like a running faucet. I needed him to taste every single drop. I can't believe that I had all that inside of me.

After it's all said and done though, I wanted him to stop. I was so drained and all I wanted to do was turn over and go to sleep. He was very persistent and continued sucking on my clit and I just keep cumming and cumming and cumming. I had multiple orgasms that night. It was so good it made my toes curl.

When I couldn't scream or cum anymore, he got off his knees and took off his boxers. Then he grabbed his penis and surprisingly, it was so hard it could barely move. When we started, I was drunk and high, but when he was done I was totally sober and felt very lightheaded.

No one had ever made me feel and respond that way sexually. Now that I was fully sober, I realized that what we'd just done wasn't right, and that I had just made the biggest mistake of my life letting him do that to me.

I knew if I didn't go through and have sex with him, he was going to be really pissed. But, I couldn't. I could not allow him to slide up inside me.

"Philip, please stop," I yelled. "I can't do this."

He's dumbfounded and asked, "Why? What's wrong? Why won't you let me finish what we started?"

I saw now that our friendship, even if anything was salvageable, was never going to be the same.

He's never going to be able to forgive me, I thought, for allowing him to eat me out and then not have sex with him.

Philip sucked his teeth. "Gabby I want you so bad. Please, can you just let nature take its course? I promise that it's going to feel good. I know that it's a lot to handle, so I'll take my time and take it slow. You don't understand just how much that I'm in love with you."

I shook my head. "Philip, can you please just get the hell up off me? Like I told you before, I can't go through with this. I know that it's going to ruin our friendship, and I'm not going to be able to live with that."

Huh, just like a man, shamelessly begging, I thought to myself. I'm not changing my mind; it's already made up.

Philip sucked his teeth and got up. And he barely said two words to me while putting on his clothes. Then he sat down on the edge of the bed, holding his head in disgust.

Philip raised his head slightly, barely looking at me with a smirk on his face. "I still can't believe that you played me like that. Now after you get what you wanted, all of a sudden you want to feel guilty. Why worry about that now when we've already crossed that bridge? We might as well go all the way. You know that you want me."

"You know what? Even if that's true, I'm not paying you any mind."

I quickly got up and started putting on my clothes. Once I was done, I sat down beside him while trying to talk some sense into him. Because now he was going to be annoying, and I didn't want to explode on him and make matters worse.

Honestly, between you and me, I could only see things going downhill from here.

I touched him on the chin and turned his face to me. "Philip, I'm sorry that you feel that way. I hope you can understand that it's for the best. I'm sorry that I even allowed it to go that far. I don't know what came over me. Nobody, and I mean nobody, has ever made me feel the way you did sexually. Nobody has ever made me cum as hard and as fast as you did. I feel like I have no worries and I can take on the world. This is Gabby's world. Right now I'm on cloud nine."

Philip looked so angry, like he wanted to snap my neck right then. The only thing that would make him feel better was hearing the words that I was going to give him some. He kept giving me dirty looks and scaring me. When he looked at me, he had the stare Jack Nicholson had when he snapped and went on the killing spree while looking for his wife in the movie *The Shining.*

Philip started hitting his head with his fists. "I can't believe this is happening to me."

Then he jumped up, walked briskly to the bathroom and slammed the door violently behind him.

I sat there for a few seconds, leaning forward, holding my hands on top of my head. I didn't know what to do or say. I thought that it was time for me to leave because I didn't know what he was capable of when he got angry. All of the time that we'd been friends, I had never seen him act like that before. I could understand that he was upset but not to that level.

It's my body and I have the right to say no whenever I choose. He couldn't force me to have sex with him.

After that, he was like a crazed fan, because we couldn't get through a conversation without him begging for sex. It became tiresome. Even six months later, when I got with my boyfriend, Gene, Philip constantly got jealous. It was like he was in competition with Gene, trying to show him up every chance he got. I foolishly thought that hooking him up with Sabrina would keep his mind occupied. It seemed like it only made things worse, like he would try to use her to make me jealous. Even doing that, he was still disrespectful in front of her and especially behind her back.

So the only other option was to distance myself and start being around him less and less. I was scared to tell Gene because he would murder Philip. He didn't play you trying to push up on his girl, while pretending to be his friend. Besides, Gene already had a record from selling drugs. I didn't think that Philip was worth my man spending time in jail.

Sooner or later, Philip is going to get exactly what he deserves. He is so arrogant and feels like he's God's gift to women. He would always say that you could be in love with two people at the same time.

I kept warning him to stop bothering me. He would stop for a while, and then go right back to it. I mean don't get me wrong, he's very attractive and all, with light green eyes and long, curly, nicely braided hair. Even though he's part Jamaican and Indian with smooth brown skin, he's still not my type. I'm more like a tomboy, so it is like hanging out with one of the boys.

Against my better judgment, I foolishly tried to give him one more chance, thinking that he could change. I was actually surprised because everything was going good for a while, but it never failed that whenever he drank, he would do it again and then beg for my forgiveness. The next day, when I would confront him about his behavior, he would say he was wasted and didn't remember a thing. I wasn't buying that excuse anymore.

I finally decided this is it! I have had enough! I called him on the phone and told him to meet me at Finnegan's, an Irish bar on Madison and 34th Street. I wanted to let him know, face to face, that it was best that we not be friends anymore, since it was obviously hard for him to handle. Everyone kept thinking something was going on with us, and frankly, I was sick of it.

Philip showed up at 7:30 that evening, and we had a couple of drinks and talked. I explained to him how the continual flirting with me was putting a strain on my friendship with Sabrina. He just looked at me, shrugged his shoulders, and acted like he didn't give a fuck. Then he stared at me like I was from another planet.

Again, he was making me feel very uncomfortable, so I just blurted it out, while looking at him eye to eye. "Didn't I tell you several times there was never going to be anything other than friendship between us?"

He paused for a few seconds, and then reluctantly nodded his head, "Yes," while sipping on his rum and Coke.

"Then, in case you haven't realized it yet, Sabrina is my sista and for that reason alone I would never sleep with you," I said. "You can be replaced, but the love and loyalty that I have for my sister is forever."

He made me feel like I was speaking a foreign language or maybe it was the effects of the alcohol. Either way, this time he had a crazy look on his face and threw me the ultimate curve ball. After all that I had said to him, he still looked at me all googley eyed and told me yet again how much he was in love with me.

I tell you, alcohol is a very dangerous thing, if it can make you act out of character that way. I was dumbfounded because Philip is not usually like that. He's more laid back.

At this point I was so angry that I just turned my back to him and completely ignored him, hoping that this time he finally got the message. Then I picked up my cell phone off the bar and started dialing my friend Peaches' number, thinking that if I didn't, I was going to explode. After two rings she answered the phone, and I started telling her about my long draining day. There was no reason for finishing the conversation with him, I was done! I'd had it! There were no more chances.

Philip sat there for about five minutes, sipping on his rum and Coke. After that, it seemed like he caught an attitude when he realized I wasn't paying him any mind. He finished his drink and then tapped me real aggressively on my shoulder. I could tell he was fuming mad because my arm felt a little tender where he tapped me. I was surprised because he had never done that before, so now I had to check him right away.

I didn't like him taking it to another level. Shit, he was not my man. And, even if he was, he still wouldn't have the right to manhandle me that way. My first instinct was to slap the shit out of him, but I held my composure because I'm a lady.

I angrily said to Peaches, "Hold on a second." I put the phone down.

I said to him, "Don't play yourself. You must be really drunk or out of your fucking mind. Don't you ever put your hands on me like that again! Just because I'm a woman, doesn't mean that I won't whip fucking ass."

He sarcastically laughed and said, "Don't play yourself." Then he stood up and continued, "Gabrielle, on everything that I love, you will regret this day for the rest of your life."

Me, being the bitch that I am, I nonchalantly turned toward him while staring at him eye to eye, laughed, picked up the phone off the bar, and then turned back and finished my conversation with Peaches.

"Okay, I didn't want to go out like this, but you've left me no choice," he said. "Bitch, get ready, because I'm going to make your life a living hell."

Then he stormed out of the bar, never once turning back. I didn't even respond to that, because I knew that he was drunk, and tomorrow he wouldn't even remember what happened.

Huh, he really fooled me that time, because soon I felt like there was a tight noose around my neck. April 1, 2007 was the beginning of my life-changing sentence. He left me hanging in mid-air. Let me tell you what this asshole did to me, despite all that he already previously put me through. Philip William Alexander spitefully went home, called Sabrina and broke up with her.

The next day, when the phone rang at six o'clock in the morning, I had a bad feeling, because nobody ever calls me at that time. It was Sabrina calling, crying hysterically, and telling me what he did to her. At that moment, I could have killed him. It took me a minute to digest, because I was still half asleep. I sat up suddenly in my bed. I felt like I had drunk ten cups of espresso coffee with an overdose of caffeine. I was out of breath and stunned at the same time. The creep only did that to her just to get back at me for refusing his sexual advances. That made me feel really bad because Sabrina didn't deserve that.

He was lucky that I'm not a violent person, because he would have gotten one straight to the head. The break-up affected her more than I expected. After that traumatic experience, I saw for the very first time, how our rock solid friendship was about to shatter like glass. I felt sick to my stomach, coughing and gasping for air. Now, after this disturbing situation, I would only be able to breathe again with friendship life support.

We were at a fork in the road, and between you and me, Sabrina was the life support that I desperately needed to stay alive. I felt immense guilt for contributing to ruining her life.

After this ordeal, Rochelle sided with Sabrina like she always does. They both became like strangers to me. I started seeing a different side to Rochelle that I'd never seen before. She always caters to Sabrina, whether it's wrong or right, and that's one of my biggest problems with her. She doesn't feel like that when it comes to Dominique and me. There was a lot of tension between all of us, and I started feeling the separation. We were no longer like the four musketeers. It was more like Cagney and Lacey and Thelma and Louise. We didn't even talk on the phone like we used to. Now surprisingly, even Rochelle started throwing me mad shade. I could just imagine the lies that she was telling Sabrina pertaining to me. What really bothers me though is that Rochelle never once took the time to even find out what my position was on the subject.

Oh well, I thought, she'll get over it. She always does. And at this point, I don't give a shit how she feels about it.

Now I saw that Rochelle couldn't be trusted either. I had to watch what I said to her about Sabrina. I guessed that whenever Sabrina felt like talking, she knew how to get in touch with me. Anyway, Rochelle needed to mind her own damn business. That's why Dominique and I are the closest, because she never gets involved, and I love that about her. She always stays neutral and never takes sides. She only listens to the situation and gives you her input if you ask for her advice. Since she was busy working on our clothing line, we would talk every other day.

What's mind blowing to me is how one event in our lives can change our relationships, as we know them, in a blink of an eye. It felt like being in the Vietnam War, and we had to be careful where we stepped because of the land mines. If we weren't careful, we would get blown up because the situation was like a big explosion waiting to happen. As a matter of fact, it had a trickling effect that was unhealthy and dangerous for all involved. After a few months of this bullshit, when Sabrina did start talking to me, I almost wished that she never spoke to me again in my life. The bitterness, and the way that she responded to me, really cut like a knife. She was constantly pushing my buttons by saying things indirectly. It didn't matter what I said to her, she would always answer me sarcastically. To be honest with you she was getting on my nerves. But since I felt guilty, I held my tongue and tried not to feed into it, although she made it very, very hard.

All of a sudden, it was like she was schizophrenic, like Sybil or something. Sabrina seemed to have developed many different personalities when it came to me. And, for the first time, she actually scared me. She's smart; she only acts crazy toward me when nobody else is around. When we were all together, she would act normal. So, when I would mention her crazy behavior, they would just think that I was hating on her. Since nobody saw her erratic behavior, no one believed me.

At one point, it appeared she was having a nervous breakdown. She started talking some crazy, off-the-wall stuff one minute, and the next minute she would act perfectly normal. I felt like I needed to take some medication or sit on somebody's couch and talk to someone. Over a period of time, she made me think that something was wrong with me. Every time I would try to reach out to her, she would be non-receptive and just push me away. Under no circumstances would she allow me to help her. She put up a wall that I couldn't even break through with a sledgehammer. This whole ordeal made me feel uncomfortable, so I just decided to take a break and stay away from her for a while.

## CHAPTER SIX

# The Challenge

Dominique, Rochelle and I became backup dancers for this hot new group, Without Extreme Prejudice, WEP for short. They were the hottest new female/male/rap/r&b group. Ramella, aka Contagious, was the female, and she has the rap style of Missy, MC Lyte, Lil' Kim, and Pepper (from Salt and Pepper), put together. Let's face it, she's dope. Jason, aka The Crypt Keeper, was laid back with the swagger of one of the best of all time, Jay Z, but with the rap style of T.I. and of Biggie Smalls, may he rest in peace.

These two artists together, in WEP, were an unstoppable force in the industry. They were selling out all over the world. And they even went triple platinum their very first time out. With us as a new addition, our shows were phenomenal. Nobody could touch us as far as dancing, especially with Dominique on our side. We practiced extra long hours every day to get us ready for our big worldwide tour.

Everyone wanted to capitalize off of the new success of Ramella and Jason. So the big companies, such as Nike, McDonald's, Wendy's, Wrigley's, Ford, and Coca-Cola, just to name a few, were offering them endorsement and advertising deals. Everyone that is anyone in the business wanted to work with them. They became the T-Pain and the Lil Wayne of the industry. WEP's success grew fast all over the world. I wasn't ready for all that. I was tired.

After three straight years on the road, on and off, I started wearing thin, and I needed a break from it all. I wanted to have kids and marry the man of my dreams. Being on the road all of the time was putting a strain on my relationship with my current boyfriend, Justin Davies. He kept telling me that he was feeling neglected, and you already know what happens then. They start to cheat. Since I was really in love with him, I was willing to make that sacrifice to save our relationship. Hell, I had only known him all my life, since the age of three, so we pretty much knew everything that there is to know about each other. Besides, all of our friends ran in the same circle, plus our families lived only two doors away from one another. What more could you ask for?

CHAPTER SEVEN

# Center Stage

Rochelle decided to try her hand at rapping once we stopped the Without Extreme Prejudice tour. That's something that she has always talked about even as a child. To be perfectly honest with you, she really has skills. From childhood she was always singing and rapping but was scared to pursue those talents for whatever reason. Now she had stars in her eyes after seeing us do our thing on the road. She was finally ready to take center stage. Rochelle wanted to make enough money so she could live a comfortable life with her three kids, Tornesha, Rosheda, and Bilal.

Bilal is the biological son of her ex-boyfriend Damien Stapleton. Damien was the starting quarterback for the New York Giants. Rochelle legally adopted Bilal after Damien was killed in a robbery gone bad. He was shot in the head by a gangbanger right in front of her as they were walking to the car. They were leaving the 40/40 Club in Atlantic City. The adoption was the right thing to do, especially since they were already living together anyway. Bilal's mother was killed in a car accident when he was three years old.

One Friday, we were at the Renaissance Club, and we met this melt-in-your-mouth, not in your hand, brother who was built like a WWF wrestler. He looked, smelled and dressed really nice. When he approached the table, none of us could take our eyes off him. He looked like he could model for *GQ* magazine.

When he started talking, he sounded like one of the characters in the Charlie Brown specials which are usually shown around Christmas time. You don't know what those characters are saying, and the only person that can understand them is Charlie Brown. It wasn't because the words that he was saying weren't clear. It was because we were all fantasizing about him. Once we all came back to reality, everything started sounding normal. Frank was getting annoyed, because he had to keep repeating himself quite a few times before we could fully understand him.

Frank smiled at Rochelle and asked, "Can I pull up a chair and sit with you ladies?"

Rochelle quickly responded. "Sure, pull up a chair." You could tell she was attracted to him.

Frank walked to the table directly behind us and grabbed a chair. Then he brought the chair back to our table and sat it down right by Rochelle.

He put his hand out and said, "Hi, my name is Frank Paige, and I'm from Power House Management. Right now I'm looking for new talent." Then he turned and looked at us. "Sorry for being so rude, but your friend…"

Rochelle cut him off in mid-sentence, and blurted out before he could even ask, "My name is Rochelle Paige…I mean Rochelle Benson." She smiled. "Sorry, I don't know what came over me. Guess that I'm a little nervous."

He smiled. "Like I was saying, she's like a Picasso painting that you put on the wall that's priceless."

Rochelle began to blush and started giggling. We looked at one another, so impressed, because nobody expected him to say that. "Thank you, that was nice of you to say," Rochelle said.

Then Frank continued, "I'm looking for talent. Can any of

you guys sing or dance?"

"Yeah, most definitely, Rochelle can," Sabrina replied.

Rochelle shyly responded, "Now you know that's not true, so why would you tell that man that?"

"Yes it is!" I said. "I thought that you wanted to be an artist. As a matter of fact, weren't you just telling me that the other day?"

Dominique chimed in. "Yeah, when we were on the road with Tek 1, I used to hear you late at night rhyming and singing those songs that you wrote. You thought that I was asleep, but I wasn't. I used to sneak and listen to all the songs you used to write and record, when you weren't around. I especially liked 'Angel,' 'Don't Play with Fire,' and 'I Don't Want to Be Lonely.'"

"You've always talked about it, so why are you acting so shy now?" Sabrina asked. "I mean really, what do you have to lose? Just go for it!"

Dominique added, "I totally agree. I second that."

Rochelle replied, "I don't know. I guess that I could give it a try."

Sabrina said they should have a toast to a new star on the rise. We all raised our glasses and toasted. Rochelle and Frank laughed and talked for hours that night. There was definitely chemistry between them.

After that night, they began dating. They hit it off so well they decided to make it official and began dating exclusively. After they were together for about a year and a half, Frank was finally able to get her to go into the studio to lay down some tracks. At first she was hesitant because she had heard a lot of horror stories from other known artists while we were on tour with Tek 1. They wound up getting ripped off and stuck in never-ending contracts that they couldn't get out of. It was like selling your soul to the devil, just for the price of fame. That happened to Tek 1 at first, until he took matters into his own hands and learned more about the business side. He introduced us to a lot of stars, and we heard their horror stories while we toured with him on the road. Back in the day, being very careful or having good people around to advise you was vital.

Most artists would try to floss and spend money way before their albums dropped. They didn't understand that every dime that a label puts out is recouped before the artist sees a dime. It happens countless times, so artists need to understand that. And the only time that the artists really make any money is if they write their own songs or they go on tour. That's why Tek 1 survived so long. He also invested his money wisely. Now he is doing movies and acting, because he realized that he couldn't continue rapping about the streets forever.

Frank told Rochelle, since she had all those concerns about the industry, that he would manage her. Then she would feel more confident and comfortable about getting into the business. Rochelle agreed to let Frank manage her even though she had a lot of insecurities and issues with trust. She told us in the beginning, it was hard for her to trust him, but after knowing him for a while, she decided to throw caution to the wind. She put it all in God's hands.

Frank kept the business side between them very professional. He got a contract drawn up and told her to take it to an entertainment lawyer. Rochelle asked us what our opinion was, and we all told her to go for it and follow her dreams. Then she also hired a family friend named Trevor Gale. He had a private practice in Manhattan. His secretary, Isabelle, called her into the office so they could discuss the contract at length. Trevor told her after viewing the contract, that the terms and percentage she would get were more than fair. He told her if she felt comfortable, then she should sign it. So that day the contract was signed.

That night, we all went out to celebrate at a club called The Lounge until 4:00 a.m. We had so much fun that night. That was the happiest that I'd seen Rochelle in a very long time. She was so anxious to get into the studio to start working on her demo that she started writing songs immediately. Every time she was around us, she was constantly practicing and letting us hear her new material. She was going to be the next big thing since Lil Kim, Foxy Brown or Queen Latifah.

About three weeks after the contract signing, Frank finally was able to secure time at one of the biggest studios in the NYC. He's really good friends with Puffy's nephew, Glover, who put in a good word for Frank, so he got a good price on the studio time. One condition was that Puffy would get the first crack at possibly signing Rochelle to a record deal. Frank felt that was more than fair, because who better to let you know if you have a hit than Puffy. He's an icon in the business.

Once Rochelle got the chance in the studio, they went hard, day and night, for the next three months, putting together a dope demo tape. Upon completion, Frank kept his promise and let Puffy hear it, but due to unfortunate circumstances and the death of Puffy's best friend and partner, Biggie Smalls, he chose to pass. He said that he was taking time off because he needed to grieve. He told Frank that maybe in the future they would be able to work together.

Frank understood and appreciated the honesty. Then he took the tape to other labels such as Island, Def Jam, Aftermath, Sony, and Warner Bros.

Rochelle had a buzz going on, so a bidding war began. Frank relentlessly went to meeting after meeting with A&R reps throughout the city. He said that he wasn't impressed with what they were offering. He didn't want to disappoint Rochelle. She got discouraged when she didn't get a chance to work with Puffy on his Bad Boy label.

A month and a half passed, so out of frustration, Frank called up his old friend Jordan Kelly. He was vice president at Milestone Records. He had started off in the mailroom, became an A&R, and then was promoted to VP. Jordan really looked out since they were old friends, and they had made a lot of money in the past. He made sure that Rochelle got a nice advance with decent points on the album.

It was a dream come true for her. Frank enlisted the hottest producers from around the world to ensure that the album was going to be sure-fire coming out of the gate. He called in a lot of favors from producers that he had dealt with in the past, so they didn't charge him much. When the album was finished six months later, everybody loved it, and it became the talk of the streets. The executives from the label wanted to throw out as much money as it took to promote it. Rochelle started doing a lot of free shows around New York, and that created a nice little buzz.

Then it was time to build an image and get Rochelle ready for the first cut off the album. Rochelle, by chance, was introduced to DJ Jazzy Joyce who was down with the VIP Record Pool at the time. Jazzy Joyce was a good friend with the pool president, Al Pizzoro, so he talked Rochelle into working with Jazzy for a little while, just until they found another DJ.

At the time Jazzy worked for 99.1 FM, a hot new rap station, doing Friday and Saturday nights from midnight to 4:00 a.m. It was hard for her to devote all of her time to the station, plus she had her side hustle, making guest appearances and DJing at different clubs throughout the NYC. When Jazzy would go on the road, a DJ by the name of Cocoa Chanelle would fill in for her. They were partners as well as co-workers.

Rochelle wrote all the songs for the album except three that her oldest daughter Rasheda wrote. Since Jazzy Joyce already had a large following, it was easy for her to market Rochelle. After about a month or so, it was time to drop the first single "Reckless." I think that Swiss Beats produced the track. Swiss knew Frank when he was down with Ruff Ryders Entertainment. Since they are good friends, he always told Frank that if he ever needed anything to give him a call.

A lot of artists made guest appearances on Rochelle's album. The industry as a whole showed her love. Jazzy Joyce had Rochelle on the radio show for two weeks straight. Rochelle did a couple of songs, rapping and singing, that her old classmate, Dawn Johnson, wrote for her back when they were in high school. She did everything a cappella. You'd be surprised how many people are actually still listening to the radio that time of night.

When her song debuted on the radio, it was an instant hit. The fans couldn't stop calling the radio show and requesting it. So naturally the other radio stations got wind of it and started playing it. They played Rochelle's song constantly for five months straight, twenty to thirty times a day.

I was sick of hearing it. I was starting to hear it in my sleep, so I stopped listening to the radio for a while. I guess that you could say that I was hating, but I would never tell Rochelle that. Everything took off fast, so Frank wanted to ride the wave and shoot a video. He talked to his cousin, Doc Rogers, who is part-ners with Hussain Winsette, an old college buddy, about shooting her video. Frank knew they did excellent work. Doc and Hussain had formed a film/video company, called H2O Films, after grad-uating from New York University's film school.

I remember the first time that Rochelle heard her song on the radio. She called me screaming at the top of her lungs. "I did it! I did it! I'm finally being played on the radio."

Frank was so proud of her that he rented a stretch Mercedes limo, and we all went out that night. Everyone was coupled up and we were heading to Club Vista on 23rd and Seventh Avenue. There were six couples, including Sabrina's favorite cousin, Courtney, who was in town visiting with her boyfriend Eddie. Courtney and Eddie were mad cool and always hung out with us when they came to New York. The whole ride in the limo, Eddie kept us laughing. He was going to be a successful come-dian. Courtney liked to draw and wanted to be a graphic artist. They were in the process of moving to New York so they fre-quently traveled back and forth. I never realized just how funny Eddie was until we saw his act when we went to visit them in Jacksonville, Florida. We caught him doing stand-up at this club called The Vintage Factory. That's where many unknown artists performed before becoming famous. I heard a lot of big names came out of there, such as Eddie Murphy, Martin Lawrence, Whoopi Goldberg, Chris Rock, Katt Williams, Monique, Sinbad, Sheryl Underwood, Capone, Simore, and Kevin Hart.

Before we actually made it to the club, we rode around for hours, watching videos and listening to Rochelle's soon-to-be-re-leased album called "Blood Money." It was one of the best nights that we had had in a long time. We were finally all together again, and it really felt good. Shit, it was a high without doing drugs.

We were all laughing and joking, when all of a sudden, everything started moving in slow motion and my brain went into taping mode. When I turned around and glanced at Sabrina, she had a very devious look on her face. That look was totally indescribable, so I couldn't put it into words. When I asked her what was wrong, she just continued to stare, not saying a word. It was like she was in a trance. I tried not to read too much into it. Besides it was Sabrina, so who was going to believe me anyway? We partied that night at Club Vista until the wee hours of the morning.

A week later, Rochelle went on tour for about three months to promote her album. After she came home, we went to two or three clubs every night. Whenever she performed, we were allowed to go backstage and meet the other artist that was out at the time. We all got the VIP treatment when we were with her, and it felt good, because I missed that from when we were dancing.

## CHAPTER EIGHT

# What Part of the Game Is This?

One day when I was on the phone with Diamond, she surprised me when she said, "Gabby, what's going on with you? You've been acting kind of strange."

I replied, "Nothing is going on. Why do you ask?"

"Well," she said, "I don't know how to tell you this, but I've been hearing nasty rumors about you."

I angrily responded, "Rumors like what?"

She hesitated at first, because she could tell in my voice that I was annoyed. "Well, for starters, I heard that you are jealous of Sabrina. Plus, you are the real reason for the break-up between her and Philip."

I couldn't hold back and yelled, "What! What the hell are you talking about? What do you mean that I'm jealous of her? You can't be serious."

She cut me off. "Wait, and let me finish. She said that you're the real reason that Philip broke up with her because you were always up in his face flirting with him. And she knows for a fact that you had sex with him. Lately, that's all she ever talks about. When I asked her why she never confronted either of you about it, she just got silent and changed the subject. She even told me that she caught you two at the Now Bar on 53rd Street and Broadway. She said that she sat and watched you and him from across the room hugging and kissing."

I couldn't believe what I was hearing. Sabrina was such a liar. Why was she lying on me like that?

"Sabrina said what hurt the most was that on this night she asked Philip if he saw or talked to you, and he blatantly lied and said no."

I couldn't believe what I was hearing, and it felt like I was in *The Twilight Zone*. I grabbed my forehead and began rubbing it. I started feeling sharp pains. I was so mystified.

This can't be happening to me, I thought.

I felt like I was being punked. I stared aimlessly out my window to see if there were some hidden trucks or cameras around. The street was deserted with only two parked cars out there. I didn't know what to make of all this. The situation was really serious. My mind was thinking crazy thoughts, so I had to calm down before I flipped out on Diamond, because that wouldn't be fair, since it had nothing to do with her.

Fuck it, I thought. I can't hold it back any longer.

I screamed at the top of my lungs; I was saying goodbye to Sabrina. I was saying that we couldn't be friends anymore, because Philip was jeopardizing my friendship with her. And trust me, he was not worth it. He was not that important to me. All I wanted was his friendship. He kept coming on to me even when they were together.

I told Sabrina that it would turn out like this and it wasn't a good idea hooking them up. She didn't want to hear that. She just wasn't listening. I should have gone with my gut feeling. I saw first-hand how he treated his girlfriend, so why would I want to put myself through that?

I kept threatening to tell Sabrina what he was doing, and he said, "Go ahead. Nobody is going to believe you."

He should have gotten an Oscar for his performance because he had everyone fooled. I waited too long, and he beat me to the punch and broke up with her. No telling what else that he was telling her. I thought that I was doing the right thing by not telling her. I should have told her because it was worse this way. I knew now that it wasn't the right decision to keep it to myself, but it was the decision that I had made at the time.

You know what surprises me though? Why she would believe him over me anyway.

We're supposed to be family, blood sisters. We've been friends for over twenty-five years and I guess that it never meant a thing.

I angrily said, "Dominique, that's just not true! You have to believe me."

Dominique said, "Calm down and stop yelling at me. I believe you, but I'm just telling you what Sabrina said. Shit, don't kill the messenger!"

She added, "Please don't say anything to her; she would kill me if she found out that I've told you. And I don't want any problems."

I responded, "I can't answer that honestly."

Diamond said, "I just felt like you should know, since she had no intention of telling you. I would expect for you to do the same for me. Look sis, if you need anything let me know. But I need for you not to say anything. I know how ornery you can be. Do I have your word?"

I reluctantly replied, after crossing my fingers. "Yes, you have my word."

"Okay, then I will talk to you later.

"Okay, I love you girl."

"I love you too."

Then we both hung up the phone. I sat there staring at a picture of all four of us. It was sitting on my dresser. It was taken when we were on tour with Tek 1 in England. We had an awesome time while we were there, with no worries.

After hanging up the phone, I kept thinking to myself about why I promised something like that to Dominique. I knew that it was something that I wasn't going to be able to do. Now I had to re-evaluate what friendship really meant to me. I was really blown away by Sabrina. She was a stranger to me. My heart was hardened to my so-called best friends. Everything that we shared together was in question.

This shit was constantly on my mind, because now being around Sabrina would be hard. I knew that she was a liar and a phony. She of all people knows that I don't fuck with people like that.

I even gave her the benefit of the doubt and hinted around to the cause of the break-up between her and Philip. She never said one word about thinking that I caused them to break up. I went so far as to ask her if she felt like I had anything to do with it, and she still said no.

I sat on the information from Dominique for months, and then when I felt like I couldn't take it anymore, I decided to go confront Sabrina face to face, woman to woman, at whatever cost. Before I did that, I went back and forth in my head repeatedly on how to face her. I kept coming up with the same conclusion that something had to be done. My reputation with my best friends was now on the line because they didn't have the balls to say what they felt to my face.

I knew I had to confront her, but unfortunately, I had no idea what I was going to say. Since I started having second thoughts about going over to her house, I figured that once I got there, I would park down the street. That would give me time to think about what to say, or how to say it.

I remember that night as if it were yesterday, because it was so humid that beads of sweat started rolling down my forehead like water running from a faucet. I could tell that I was nervous, because I don't usually sweat. When I looked down at my clothes, I was totally soaked. As I was driving, I glanced at the clock and it read 9:00 p.m., so I figured that she would definitely be home, because on Wednesday nights she likes to watch *Law and Order* that comes on at that time.

I reached Sabrina's street and parked. I waited a few seconds, and then I opened the door with great hesitation and got out of the car. Since I didn't know how Sabrina was going to respond, I started walking slowly to try to get my thoughts together. And just as I was walking up the block, a black Lexus SUV with tinted windows pulled up in front of her house. For some reason, the car looked very familiar. It was hard to see inside the Lexus, due to the dark windows and dark night.

I wondered, "Who the hell is in there?"

Being nosy, I stopped suddenly in my tracks and crouched down behind a tree so I could get a better look without being noticed. I could hear the song by Beyonce called "All the Single Ladies." It was playing so loudly that I imagined the glass was going to shatter. Seconds later, someone rolled down the windows of the Lexus. Then I heard talking, very faintly, coming from the SUV. I still was too far away to hear clearly.

All of a sudden I realized it was the voices of a man and a

lady. I wanted to get closer without being detected, so I carefully tip-toed to a tree that is in the yard next to Sabrina's house. Now I could hear better, while getting a much closer look. The longer that it took for whomever it was to get out of the vehicle, the more curious I became. They say that sometimes curiosity kills the cat, and it can just be better not knowing.

Oh well, this was one of those times that I should have minded my own business. I stood in one spot, intrigued and full of anticipation. About two minutes later, the engine stopped. Right away, the passenger side door swung open and I could hear a lot of laughing, because of the windows being down. I'm waiting and waiting and waiting. Still nothing. I wished they would hurry up and get out of the goddamn car. I started to get a cramp in my legs from being crouched down in one position.

Now look what the hell is coming my way, I thought. I can't believe this. It's a goddamn German Shepherd. What the hell is he doing out here this time of night? I guess he's looking for food. Shit, he doesn't even have a leash on and no owner walking behind him. Now I can't move even if I wanted too. I don't want to give myself away. I have to say a prayer and hope that he goes away.

I have a fear of dogs, thanks to my brother Marcus. He used to chase me around the house with our dog Shadow. One time he told Shadow to attack me, and the dog bit me. He didn't break the skin. My father had to get rid of him for biting me. Shit, I was finally going to teach Marcus a lesson. I made such a stink about the bite, so it was going to be Shadow or me. You know I'm daddy's little girl, so Shadow had to go. Marcus was pissed, but so what? He shouldn't have done that. I kept telling him to stop bothering me and he wouldn't listen. I was tired of all his abuse.

Suddenly someone got out of the passenger door and stood on the sidewalk, while slightly turning toward me. Since it was dark, it was hard for me to see. The person that got out of the Lexus kind of resembled Sabrina, but I couldn't be sure at the time.

If she turns a little bit more into the light, I thought, I can see her face a little better.

The dog started barking behind her, and it scared her, so she turned her head toward the light, and I was finally able to see her face.

*Oh my God, it's Sabrina! Now let's see who the mystery man is.*

I was not ready for what I was about to discover next. The driver's side door opened slowly. A light-skinned man, very muscular, emerged wearing a crisp wife-beater with gray and white plaid shorts. As he closed the door, he walked around the Lexus into the light, holding a dozen roses in his hands. He stopped right in front of Sabrina and gave her a passionate kiss on the lips for about fifteen seconds. Then they embraced in a hug, and that's when I saw his face.

I thought, Oh…MY…God…it's Rochelle's boyfriend, Mike! I cannot believe this. What are they doing?

I was about to vomit, so I put my hand over my mouth. Now I was definitely not going anywhere. I had to hear what was going on. I wished that I had a tape recorder. I could use it to blackmail her, and now my revenge would be bittersweet.

I'm not going to let her get away with this, I thought. Wait a minute! Let me see what they're saying.

Mike said, "Sabrina I had a lot of fun but I have to be going now. I have to go pick the kids up at the babysitter's house before it gets too late."

Sabrina pleaded, "Oh please, just come in for a few minutes. It's not even nine o'clock yet, so you still have time." Then she laughed. "I won't tell if you won't tell. Trust me. Nobody is going to find out about this. I know how to keep a secret. I do this all the time. Rochelle is thousands of miles away. Do you know what she's doing while she's on the road?"

Mike shook his head "No." He grabbed Sabrina's hands, and then they turned to one another and embraced in a passionate kiss. I slapped myself, because I thought that I was dreaming. I opened and closed my eyes quickly, twice, just to make sure. When I opened my eyes, it was the real deal.

I thought to myself…You know what? She has a lot of fucking nerve, especially since she has been talking mad shit about me behind my back. Then she turns around and does something like this to Rochelle. I can't believe that Rochelle took Sabrina's side over mine. She should have stayed neutral and stayed out of it, because it's normal for sisters to have fights and disagreements. How could Sabrina do this to Rochelle?

I knew that when Rochelle found out what they were doing behind her back, she was going to feel like an asshole. My mouth dropped and I felt sick to my stomach, so I held myself up with one hand while leaning on the tree. Then I crouched over and started vomiting my guts out, until there was nothing left inside.

Hell, if Sabrina could do that to Rochelle, then there was no telling what she could do to us. Rochelle had been with her boyfriend for about two years, after the mutual break-up between her and Frank.

I'm so disgusted, I thought, so to hell with talking to her about what I originally came over here for. If I talk to her now, I'm going to slap her in the face and try to knock her teeth down her throat. I can't take seeing this anymore. She's a hypocrite.

Now I was ready to go back to my car because I felt weak. Anyway, what can you expect? A man is going to be a man. I just wouldn't have expected that from Mike. After they stood outside kissing, they finally went inside, and that's when I staggered to my car. I sat in my car for five minutes trying to decide what to do.

I was thinking that from this day on, even though it has nothing to do with me, I had no respect for Sabrina. I knew the right thing to do was to call Rochelle up on the phone and let her know what Sabrina was doing.

But on second thought, what if I told her, and she didn't believe me?

Shit, I thought, she's on the road promoting her album. You can't tell someone something like that over the phone. She would really hate me then. She would cancel the rest of her shows and get back to the states on the first thing smoking. Then Rochelle would unleash a massive can of whip-ass on Sabrina. Believe me, she would deserve it! I don't know how I would feel about finding out the truth if I was Rochelle. I guess that I would be totally devastated and hurt.

I decided to wait awhile before saying anything and weigh my options. I was getting a headache, so I just started up the car and pulled off. As I was driving past her house, I saw the German Shepherd out the corner of my eye about to run across the street right in front of my car. Then I looked to my left and Sabrina came walking out her door.

"Oh, shit, I'm fucked," I said.

She walked over to her car and was about to open the door with the key.

"Shit!" I said. "Let me drive slowly past her house and maybe she won't notice me. What the fuck!"

Here came the crazy-ass dog again, and he was about to run across the street. When I blew my horn at the dog, Sabrina looked at my car. I tried to hide my face, but it was way too late. She saw me. She looked dead in my face. She frowned and gave me that disturbed look again. I sped past her house and raced down the block. I barely stopped at the red light before quickly turning right at the corner.

CHAPTER NINE

# What's the 411? Introducing Mary J. Blige

When Rochelle was not on the road, she worked at a local radio station WMRZ. She got in there with the help of a woman named Angie Martinez who had been there for a long time. Angie really liked Rochelle a lot, so she took her under her wing. Rochelle was her intern but had plans on becoming a radio show host. Angie taught her the ins and outs of the business. I guess that you could say Rochelle was her protégée. Anyway, we had all made plans to hang out and go to this big industry party, featuring Mary J. Blige, one of my favorite performers of all time. After three successful albums, Mary was ready to celebrate dropping a fourth, and I wanted to be there.

I was trying to figure out how I was going to be able to avoid Sabrina in a public place during the party. She was going to push up on me extra hard trying to convince me not to expose the tramp and the liar that she was. It was getting to the point that friendship didn't have the meaning that it used to.

I was going to try my best to avoid her, but I knew it was going to be hard. Maybe if I stayed drunk all night, she'd stay away from me. She doesn't like how I respond to people sometimes when I drink.

Four days had passed since I had seen Sabrina and Mike, and I was nervous about seeing Rochelle for the first time in months. When she would come back in town for a day or two, I wouldn't be able to see her because if she wasn't home, she was at the station. Prior to that, she was on tour with the two hottest female DJs in the NYC, MK and Kim B. They met her through mutual friends of ours—Sophina, Kate and Dot—who all work for the club, Lover Girls, on Seventh Avenue and 23rd Street. Sophina is one of the managers, and Dot is one of the bouncers. Kate is the promoter for the club.

Finally, it was the day of the album release party, and I was so excited. Everyone that is *anyone* was there. They were all sitting in the VIP section. I saw Puffy, Lil Kim, Missy, Ciara, Keisha Cole, Tank, LL Cool J, Jay-Z, Beyonce, and Salt and Pepper. Sitting in the corner, I saw Oprah and Gayle talking to radio host Ed Lover, Déjà Vu, and Big Boi. The DJs that were making guest appearances were: Mister C, Funk Master Flex, Marley Marl, Jazzy Joyce, Cocoa Chanelle, and Kool DJ Red Alert. The crowd was out of control. It was so packed in there that you could barely move.

The minute Mary started her show, the crowd was captivated. She was blowing us away. She took control and showed everyone why she is the Queen of Hip-Hop Soul. While she was on stage singing, her friends made guest appearances. They performed some of her biggest hits. She sings so great that she got top names to work with her, such as Fifty Cent, Method Man, Dr. Dre, Jay-Z, Puffy, and Missy. They all killed it. With all those people helping out, she didn't need anyone to open up for her.

After she finished the last song, the crowd went wild. They kept calling her back for an encore. I love her because she is so graceful. She didn't let it go to her head. She kept thanking the crowd for all of their support over the years. That night, she said, she really felt the love that the NYC was giving.

She was on stage easily for about three hours with all the guest appearances and the stage show that she put together. During the show, she played a mini-film of past performances, while sharing countless interviews. They even had footage of her on the road and in the studio working on the songs for her upcoming albums. After she performed the last song, "Street Life," with Jadakiss from the Lox, she ran off stage and hugged her boyfriend Tony. Then she hugged her two managers that have stuck it out with her over the years, Rick and Gene.

Rochelle had backstage passes, so we actually got the chance to meet Mary in person. When we entered the room, she was talking to Angie and her other close friend, Gladys Knight, another icon. About five minutes later, there was a faint knock on the door. Guess who walked in but Michael Shawn and DJ Envy from the All Access morning show? They popped in to congratulate Mary on the outstanding performance. They walked over to her, smiling, and gave her a hug and a kiss on the cheek.

DJ Envy said, "Mary, I would like to invite you up to the show so you can promote your new album. Also, I would like to out you on my new mixed tape that's about to drop at the end of the month."

Mary replied, "Sure, I love you guys. I would be more than happy to come up to the station. Besides, I have some promotional stuff to give you. You show Mary much love."

Michael laughed and whispered to Envy, "Maybe you better clear it with Tasha first."

Envy waved him off and said, "Mike, no, that won't be necessary." Envy worked with Tasha, who was called Miss Jones on air. Envy knew Tasha was Mary's number one fan.

Before they left, Michael Shawn said, "Mary, call us, and let us know when you're coming up to the station." Then the door slammed behind them.

## CHAPTER TEN

# The Set Up! Sabrina's Revenge

The next day, I heard three knocks on the door and it startled me. I had fallen asleep in my usual spot on the couch. I spend more time on the couch than in my own bed. The TV is always watching me. Anyway, when I looked at my watch, it read 10:15 p.m. I know that I'm not expecting anyone, and I'm a very private person. If you decide that you just want to pop up at my house, unannounced, then you won't get in. Whoever was there was really persistent and kept ringing the doorbell and knocking on my door. Just out of curiosity, I crept over to the door and looked out the peephole.

"Shit, it's Sabrina," I said aloud. "What the hell does she want? I don't feel like dealing with her bullshit right now, so she's going to have to wait."

She rings the doorbell, three more times. Well, needless to say, I didn't even care. And I left her fucking ass standing out there. I used the bathroom and I carried my ass upstairs and went to bed. Next thing I knew, about an hour later, my cell phone started ringing. I picked up the phone and looked to see who was calling before answering. Damn, if it wasn't Sabrina blowing up my phone calling me back to back. She was really getting on my nerves. I was about to let her have it. The phone kept ringing so much that I couldn't go back to sleep. I kept looking at the clock, on and off. I was so tired because of the constant calling, and I couldn't even tell you the countless times that she went from my cell phone to my house phone.

If I don't get my beauty rest for tomorrow, I thought, I'm going to look a hot mess. And I can't have that; I have a reputation to uphold. She's acting like a stalker.

She had to be sitting outside my house, because the doorbell was ringing off the hook. I was tired and pissed, so I angrily put on my slippers and went downstairs. I quietly tip-toed over to the door, and again I saw Sabrina standing there.

This bitch is really trying to play me close, I thought. She should have already gotten the hint that I'm not fucking with her like that anymore. She's about to catch a bad decision. It's like she's trying to force me to talk to her and I can't stand that. I hate when she gets like that. It's annoying.

Since I didn't answer the door, she started screaming my name at the top of her lungs. "Gabby! Gabby! It's me Sabrina!"

She sounded like she was drinking because she was slurring her words. She paused and then said, "I know that you're in there. I see your car in the driveway, and all your lights are on. This time, rest assured, I'm not leaving until you open this door and talk to me woman to woman. All I want to do is talk to you like an adult. You seriously need to stop acting like a child. I'm feeling slighted and ignored. At the album release party, you talked to everyone but me. I've been calling your house phone and your cell phone to no avail. So, now this is my only other option, to resort to something like this. You are my sister and I love you. I really need you right now. Please don't shut me out."

That bitch doesn't know the meaning of friendship or love, I thought.

After hearing her say that, she pissed me off even more, so I just left her standing out there, yet again. I went upstairs to the bathroom and then took my ass back to bed. After standing outside for over half an hour, she finally got the hint and left.

## CHAPTER ELEVEN

# Rochelle, the Show Stopper

A few weeks had gone by, and it was the day of Rochelle's album release party. I wasn't feeling good, plus I was tired from partying with Dominique and my boyfriend, Jared, the night before. I had to literally drag myself out of the bed.

I was trying to think of an excuse to miss the party, so I didn't have to deal with Sabrina that night. But then I thought of how that wouldn't be fair to Rochelle, because it was going to be one of her biggest nights. She would be mad if I wasn't there.

So after dragging around for a few hours, I finally got my ass moving. I jumped in the shower, got dressed and went to Fenton's Department store on 125th to look for an outfit. I left the house around 6:45 and soon arrived at the Elite Club on 23rd and Sixth Avenue. As I pulled up in my white Escalade, I could see people lining up to go inside. I wanted to get there early because that would give me a chance to unwind before the girls got there.

There were six bouncers, four men and two women. They were standing around in a circle, talking and laughing. Two of the men were stocky and two looked like model types. One of them had a close shaven head and the other one had nice long dread locks. One of the females was tall and slender, with her hair pulled back in a ponytail, and the other one looked more aggressive with a low-cut hairstyle.

If your name wasn't on the guest list, you weren't getting in. They also had two undercover police officers standing outside, just in case anything jumped off. Since this was a big event, the label did not want to take any chances, because they had invested a lot in Rochelle. She was a big money maker for the label, and all of her shows were selling out. After about ten minutes of looking for a park, I decided to use the valet service. So I pulled up in front of the club, and the valet guy opened the door, wrote me a ticket and said to enjoy.

I said thanks, and got out of the car and walked to the long line. I waited about fifteen minutes and finally went inside.

The club was big and looked real nice. The DJ was pumping a Busta Rhymes song. So far it was a nice little crowd. People stopped and stared at me as I made my way across the room to the bar. It was strange to me, because I don't like a lot of attention. All of the attention was coming because I was wearing this fly black dress made by Enyce.

I'm plain Jane. I'm usually wearing jeans and slacks, boots and sneakers. I saw that I stuck out like a sore thumb. (Everyone tells me that I have natural beauty.) Once I got a seat at the bar, I called the bartender over to order me a Cosmopolitan. If I had a few drinks in me, at least it would take the edge off. Then I would be able to deal with that bitch Sabrina.

About twenty to thirty minutes and a few drinks later, Dominique showed up in a stunning new outfit that she designed. As soon as she entered the room, people were impressed with the outfit she was wearing. They kept stopping and complimenting her like she was a star. After a few minutes, she finally made her way over to me at the bar. I was on my third drink. I was tipsy, so now I was ready to deal with Sabrina.

At the bar, Diamond sat down next to me and ordered an apple martini and a bottle of Dom Perignon with two champagne glasses. Usually, throughout the night, we bought each other drinks. If someone that we were attracted to didn't buy us drinks, it really didn't matter, because we stayed with money. We always attracted men with money, ballers with good jobs. And they would buy us drinks all night because they were trying to get in our pants. Just because they spend their money it doesn't mean that they are getting in our pants, because we don't play that. If we really like them, we would give them some play; otherwise, they would be dismissed at the end of the night, after buying us drinks all night. More than likely we wouldn't ever see them again, because we never really frequent the same club too often.

I wished Sabrina wasn't coming, but I knew that she was not going to miss this for the world. She already knew it was the only way that she was going to be able to talk to me face to face or otherwise.

Forty-five minutes later, the skank Sabrina arrived. The club was so packed and you could barely move without bumping into someone. The lights flashed on and off several times.

Then DJ Amere got on the mic and said, "Hello everyone. Thanks for coming out to album release party for Luscious. I hope that you're having a good time. We're going to do things a little different tonight. In a few minutes Luscious is going to come out to perform a few of songs. There are a lot of special guests and fans in the house tonight. Now, until the show starts just enjoy the sounds of me, DJ Amere. You can hear me every night Monday through Friday on WMRZ from 6:00 to 10:00 p.m. Tonight, I'll be spinning the latest hits in hip-hop. You know how I do and I get down. So let's get this party started off right with a song from Luscious."

He put on Rochelle's song, "Reckless," and the crowd went crazy. Then he started mixing in some of her other songs. I love DJ Amere. He's got skills. He's the best-kept secret and he does the rush hour segment. Wherever he plays, he gets paid, especially, because he's down with the Hit Squad. Since he was good friends with Rochelle's boyfriend, Mike, he did the show for nothing.

As I was coming from the bathroom, I ran into Ramella and Jason. So I brought them over to where we were sitting at the bar, and we had a few drinks together. I knew that they were glad to be home, because they'd just gotten off a big thirty-city tour. They asked Diamond and me to come and dance for them again. Me, myself, I'd had enough of being on the road. Besides I liked my privacy. I enjoyed being around my family and friends. Even though I was with my girlz, I still missed my boo. Jason was always telling Diamond and me that he and Ramella were going to get into acting for film and television.

I told Jason and Ramella that we wanted to sit down with them and discuss their backing our clothing line, "Unique Expressions." Ramella was ecstatic that we even considered them. We agreed that Diamond and I would meet up with them that following Monday, and we could work out a deal for financial backing.

They were always impressed by Diamond's designs, so I was confident that something could be worked out. I think Jason had a crush on Diamond, because I would always catch him staring at her. The outfit that she had on that night was so fly that I guess Jason couldn't resist looking at her from head to toe. One thing that I can say about Diamond is that she is well put together.

Luckily, that night, Diamond brought her portfolio to the party. When she showed them some of the sketches, Jason and

Ramella were so impressed. Jason said they would get a contract drawn up by their lawyer, so we could have someone look it over for us. Then if everything was okay, we could meet them at their office on 42nd Street and finalize things.

Jason ordered three bottles of champagne to celebrate. We all held up our glasses and he said, "Here's to new beginnings and partnerships." Then we all shook hands and partied until the show began.

Thirty minutes later, the lights flashed on and off three times. Seconds later, Big Tigga from "Live in the Den" appeared on stage and asked, "Can I get everyone's attention?"

Everyone stopped what they were doing and turned toward the stage. Tigga continued in his raspy voice, "How's everyone doing tonight?"

He was dressed very casually with a nice pair of Sean John jeans with a fly Coolio sweater and a black fitted hat to match.

The crowd responded, "We are doing fine!"

Then he said, "Well then, I would like to introduce myself. For those who don't know me, my name is Big Tigga from 'Live in the Den.' You have also seen me on BET'S 'Live in the Basement.'"

The crowd started cheering and said, "We love you, Tigga!" After that, the audience clapped for thirty seconds non-stop.

Tigga blushed. "I love you guys too. Thanks for all the support that you have given me all these years in my endeavors. But it's not about me tonight. I'm not the one that you are here to see. You are here for Luscious' album release party. And trust me, this album is so hot. Every track on this album is thumping. I honestly think that she's going to be around for many years to come. Tonight, we have a very big line of other artists that are here to help kick this party off right. Everyone put your hands together for DJ Amere on the ones and twos."

The crowd clapped. "Now before we get started, without further ado, here's Luscious!"

When Luscious walked out on stage, the crowd went wild. I was so proud of her because this was something that she had wanted to do since she was a child.

Rochelle walked over to Tigga and gave him a hug. He turned to the crowd and said, "This is a very dear friend of mine, and I love her to death. So let's get this party started. This I promise you…it's going to be a night that you won't soon forget!"

The lights went off slowly, Tigga ran offstage, and Rochelle followed him. About ten seconds later, we heard a loud, crackling noise that sounded like gunshots, with sparks coming out of the floor. In the background, you heard Missy Elliot's voice singing one of her hit songs "Ching A Ling." As the lights came back on, Missy ran on stage. Then Rochelle followed behind her, and they gave each other a hug and a kiss on the cheek.

As the music got louder, you could hear Missy singing the intro to her song. She repeated it twice. While she was saying it the second time, four females, two from each side, danced on the stage. Then they rotated around Missy and Rochelle. After that, four male dancers, two on each side, danced on stage doing something different, but they were all in sync with each other. Way in the back MK and Kim B were hyping up the crowd. Then you heard Missy singing the hook of the song. That was when the crowd went wild.

The audience did not expect for Missy to come out and show support for Rochelle and do a song with her. All the dancers were dancing in sync, and Missy and Rochelle were doing their own rehearsed steps. They were also singing the background lyrics.

Once the song was finished, the crowd went crazy, cheering and clapping.

Missy said, "Thank you, I love you guys! I'd like to thank Luscious for letting me come on stage and perform with her tonight." Then she gave Rochelle a pound and ran off stage.

MK and Kim B said, "Let's have a round of applause for Missy!" The crowd clapped continuously for several minutes. Then MK started playing the background music for the new song, "Don't Play with Fire," off Rochelle's album.

Next, a female voice began singing the intro, as Rochelle and the dancers began their fly dance routine. Rochelle moved like Michael Jackson at the height of his career. She was smooth as she glided across the stage, in sync with her dancers. When she began to rap and sing, it captivated the audience. She tore the place down.

The outfits that she wore that night were awesome. Dominique had designed them for our clothing line. Once the word got out about our clothing, people were buying it like crazy. Rochelle always made a point of letting people know about the line and that they should support us. After that, it became the new trend in urban gear because of her. Other stars started rocking our gear and that only added to our credibility. I guess it caught on because it's affordable to the average consumer.

When Rochelle finished her set, she received a standing ovation. Everyone was clapping and screaming her name. People started snapping pictures left and right. And from the ceiling, money started falling. It was fifties, hundreds, tens, fives, and dollar bills all in the color red.

After that, Rochelle ripped it and did one final song called "Blood Money," with Jadakiss and Styles P from The LOX. Their stage presence together was totally awesome. Jadakiss and Styles P came straight out of Yonkers. They were the hottest rappers, besides DMX, coming out of Yonkers.

The song was so contagious that the crowd didn't know what to do. Rochelle had the whole place singing the hook and dancing. When the song was finally finished, Jadakiss and Styles P gave Rochelle a kiss and thanked her for allowing them to make a guest appearance with her. Then they said goodbye to the crowd and walked off the stage. Rochelle thanked everyone for coming. She turned toward Kim B, MK, and the dancers and thanked them as well. She blew the crowd a kiss and ran off stage. MK and Kim B started playing background music, the dancers danced their way off stage, one by one, and the lights slowly went down. This was one of the best performances that I had seen, outside of the last concert that we had seen with MJB. Everyone seemed as though they really liked Rochelle's performance.

After that, Big Tigga came back on stage with his mic in his hand and said, "Girlfriend, you have arrived. I'm very proud of you. Now everyone put your hands together and give her a big round of applause!" The applause went on and on.

About forty-five minutes later, Rochelle, MK and Kim B made their way to the bar where we were sitting, and we embraced them.

"I'm glad that it's over, because I was so nervous!" exclaimed Rochelle.

MK said, "Girl, you performed like a pro. Don't worry about a thing when you're out there. We got your back."

"Yeah, they can't see us!" said Kim B. "We are about to take this industry by a storm lyrically and musically!"

They all laughed and gave each other a pound. Rochelle turned to MK and Kim B and said, "I really appreciate you guys, and I know that I couldn't have done this without you. I love you both. You kept the crowd going and you really hyped me up."

Kim smiled. "That's what we get paid for—crowd control and keeping things moving. We've only been doing this DJ thing for about fifteen years.

MK stood up. "Now let's have a toast to our success and also to all the haters out there!"

People kept coming up to let them know how good their performance was. An editor named Selena Johnson from *Hip Hop* magazine came over to them and wanted to do an interview for an upcoming issue. MK, Kim B, and Rochelle walked off with her and a photographer to a more secluded area.

I felt as though someone was staring at me, and when I looked out of the corner of my eye, I noticed it was Sabrina. She had an indescribable look on her face. At this point, I really didn't pay her any mind because I was so wasted.

Diamond said, "Are you okay? You look like you are out of it."

I guess my facial expression said it all. "Girl, I'm wasted," I replied. "I was mixing my drinks, which I never really did before. I don't know how I'm going to get home, because I'm in no condition to drive. So I'm going to do the responsible thing and leave my car here and take a cab home, unless you're willing to give me a ride home. That would be even better."

I was trying to say this low so Sabrina wouldn't hear me, because I knew that she would offer to take me home, just to be able to talk to me. Hell, I didn't want that. I had done a good job of avoiding her all night. Every time she approached me, I quickly got up and danced or pretended like I was about to make a phone call.

I turned to Dominique. "Can you please give me a ride home, and I will leave my car here? Or if you can't, I will just take a cab home."

I didn't even know that Sabrina was listening to our conversation, since she was busy talking on the phone. She quickly responded before Diamond could even say a word. "Oh Gabby, I'll drive you home in your car, and then I will take a cab home from your house since we don't live that far away from one another."

"No, that's okay," I answered. "I will just leave my car here and take a cab home. I don't want to inconvenience you."

Sabrina frowned. "What are you talking about, girl? Don't be silly. It's no trouble at all. I just want to make sure that you make it home okay. Besides, that's what friends are for. Plus, we can catch up on what's been going on in each other's lives. I haven't been able to catch up to you lately. You haven't been answering your phone."

The next thing that I knew, everything became a blur, and after that, I really didn't remember a thing. I'm pretty sure that I passed out. When I woke up the next morning, the clothes that I had on the night before were off. I was just wearing a cut-off shirt and my sexy red thong with my initials on it. All of my underwear are customized with either my name or my initials. I was lying in my bed with the cover pulled up over my head. I had a splitting headache; my head was pounding. I could have sworn that I was still drunk, because it felt like the room was spinning. I felt sick and didn't want to get out of bed.

When I looked down on the floor, I noticed the clothes that I'd had on the night before were thrown around the room. My Louis Vuitton bag was in the corner turned upside down. I turned on the radio, and I heard Miss Jones from the morning show talking about Rochelle's slamming performance the night before. She said that she really enjoyed her show. She was asking all the listeners that saw Rochelle's performance to call in and give their comments. Then she played excerpts from the performance while Michael Shawn gave Rochelle praise. They said that she was a breath of fresh air, something new and crisp.

Michael Shawn is so X-rated and always has something funny to say. He was telling Miss Jones that he had the matchstick that would light Rochelle's fire. I began to laugh because he was saying that in reference to her new song, "Don't Play with Fire."

Just then the phone rang and it startled me. I wasn't expecting anyone to call me so early in the morning. I didn't even feel like answering the phone, I just wanted to be left alone. When I looked at the clock on the nightstand, it read 5:30. That annoyed me, so I decided to let the answering machine pick it up. After listening to the message, if it were important enough, then I would call them back or catch the call before it hung up. My answering machine announced the person's number, because I have call reject.

I said to myself as I was listening to the number, "Oh shit, it's Rochelle." I could barely understand her. She was crying uncontrollably. So I jumped out of bed and almost tripped over my shoes that were carelessly lying on the ground. I was trying to pick up the phone before she hung up. I have never moved so fast in my life. I was able to catch it on the last ring, and I had to take a minute or two to catch my breath.

Then as I was walking back over to my bed, I asked in a very nervous voice, "Hello, Rochelle. What's wrong?"

Rochelle replied, "I can't believe that this has happened to me!"

"What can't you believe? What's going on?" I sat down on the end of the bed, and then I continued, "Just calm down, take a deep breath and tell me what happened."

"Someone stole my money."

I froze for a few seconds. "Rochelle, what did you say?"

She repeated it, angrier this time. "You heard me. Someone stole my money."

It still didn't compute in my mind and I was so confused. That word didn't come up in our vocabulary. I was tongue-tied and I couldn't seem to get my thoughts together. I was finally able to reply after it took almost a minute to register.

"How could anyone steal your money? Did someone rob you at gunpoint?"

I knew it was a dumb question to ask, especially at the moment. The words came out of my mouth, before I had a chance to think about it. Actually, I didn't know what to say, but I didn't want her to think that I wasn't listening or wasn't concerned.

"No silly," she snapped. "I had the money in my purse and someone went into my purse and took the money. And that's what bothers me so much. As I remember correctly, my purse was sitting right next to you at the end of the bar."

I said, while scratching my head, "I don't remember seeing your purse sitting next to me. To tell you the truth, I don't remember too much about last night."

Even Rochelle's performance was a little blurry to me. She said, "Yeah, remember when I came out after doing the show, I asked you to watch it when the editor came over to me at the bar wanting to interview me? She wanted to take a picture, so we went somewhere quieter."

I sighed. "I still don't remember that, but how much was taken?"

"Five hundred dollars."

"I'm sorry to hear that Rochelle, but unfortunately, I still don't remember. I guess that I was out of it. I don't even remember how the hell that I got home last night. I didn't see anyone going into your purse."

Before I could say another word, Rochelle cut me off and said, "The two things in the world that I can't stand are a liar and a thief."

"Well," I snapped, "are you trying to imply that I took your money?"

"No. Hell no, why would you think that? I already know that you wouldn't steal from me. I'm telling you, Gabby, whoever took my money, God help them. Because when I find out who it is, they will be dealt with, I promise you that. You already know how I get down, need I say more? Shit, I work hard for my money, and nobody has the right to take it from me. Everybody knows that I would give it to you if you asked me for it. I'm a very generous person. It makes me mad to know that I'm around a loser like that. I was drunk, but I know exactly how much money that I had on me. I guess they figured that it would go unnoticed, since I had a lot of money on me. Anyone that knows me knows I always keep large amounts of money for emergencies that might arise. You know that I roll deep. Never in my life have I experienced something like this before. It's not a good feeling and makes me very sad."

"Are you sure that you didn't make a mistake?'

Rochelle responded sarcastically, "I'm not a dummy! I know how to count, and I know how much money that I have on me at all times. I hope I never find out who did it."

"Don't worry," I said. "What goes around comes back around.

Karma is a bitch."

"I guess that you're right."

"Girl, I have a massive headache, so I will call you back later."

"I love you, Gabby."

"I love you too."

We always tried to say that before we hung up the phone. Then I went back to sleep to try to get rid of the hangover.

## CHAPTER TWELVE

# Sabrina, the "Black Widow"

Later on that evening, around six, I heard a loud knock on the door. It scared me, so I jumped out of my sleep. I walked downstairs very slowly, because I was still sleepy and hung over. Just as I got to the door, I heard three more knocks on the door, back to back. I looked through the peephole.

"Oh shit, it's Sabrina again."

She was wearing a gray Baby Phat sweat suit with gray and blue New Balance sneakers.

She anxiously said, "Gabby, it's me, Sabrina. Open the door."

I dropped my head and looked down on the floor, while putting my hand on my forehead. I took a long deep breath and shook my head in disgust. Now, I was definitely wide awake. I thought to myself that I couldn't keep running from her, because sooner or later, I was going to have to deal with the situation. She kept being persistent and obviously was not going to let this shit go. And like my mother always told me, "Easy is better than hard."

I took another deep breath and slowly opened the door with a phony smile on my face. "Sabrina what are you doing here?"

"I came to see if you were okay. I mean the other day when I brought you home from the album release party, you were out of it. I've never seen you act like that before. You kept fighting me when I was trying to take your clothes off. You were a total mess. You kept throwing up. After I cleaned you up, you started crying and grabbing on me. You kept calling Rochelle's name and saying how much you loved her. Then, the strange thing was you kept saying, 'I'm sorry Rochelle. I didn't mean to do it. So, can you please find it in your heart to forgive me? And I will never let this happen again.' I was trying to figure out why you said that, but I just chalked it up to you being drunk and paid it no mind."

She stood right in front of me and gave me a fake hug and a kiss on the cheek. Then she asked, "Aren't you going to let me in? I mean, where are your manners?"

"Yeah, of course, come right in. You know that you're welcome here day and night." I moved to the right. "Come in, and don't be silly."

When she walked in, a strange feeling that I never felt before came over me. It felt as if I was just meeting her for the first time, and she couldn't be trusted. I closed the door and said, "Please have a seat on the couch."

Then she sat down while crossing her legs. "Girl, you look like you've seen a ghost."

"No, I just have a headache, and my head has been pounding all day. I tried to sleep it off, but when I wake up, it just seems to come back even stronger. Plus, the goddamned phone keeps ringing, so eventually I just turned it off."

Then I asked her if she was hungry or needed anything from the kitchen.

"No thanks. I'm trying to preserve my girlish figure," she replied. "My mother told me I was getting fat. Besides, I had a slice of pizza with pepperoni before I came over here."

I went into the kitchen and took two Advil with a glass of

water. I stood there for a few seconds, and thought about how I was dreading going back into the living room, but there was no way to get around it.

I braced myself and walked back in there. Sabrina had the cable remote in her hands and was flipping through the channels. She stopped when she reached that hit show on HBO called *Big Love,* a show that deals with polygamy. It's about this guy that has three wives living next to each other and they are all friends. I guess that's why she could relate to the show.

I stood there in the doorway for a minute, just staring at her. Then I walked over and sat down in my comfortable reclining chair. Most of the time I would fall asleep in that chair while watching TV.

At this point I felt kind of tense, so I asked, "Sabrina, what's good?"

"You have been avoiding me. I've been waiting patiently to talk to you face to face for weeks now. And if I didn't know any better, I would honestly believe that you were trying to avoid me."

I looked right at her because now it was very crucial to know what my response was going to be.

Yeah, I thought, you are not all beauty and no brains, huh?

Then I sat up straight and replied, "No. Why would you ever think something like that?"

"Well, I don't really know," she said with a sneaky grin on her face. "I've tried my damnedest to figure that out. I mean we haven't argued or anything, but all I know is, you've been acting really strange towards me lately. Have I done anything to you?"

I said, with a fake-ass smile, "I don't understand where you are coming from with this. I have barely seen you. Matter of fact, this is the first time that I've seen you since the album release party."

Sabrina put the remote control down on the table in front of her, and leaned forward. Then she put her purse down beside her. "Is there something going on with you? You know that you are my sister, and we've been through thick and thin. You know that I've always had your back no matter what, right?"

I sarcastically responded, "There is nothing to talk about. Everything is okay. I've just been feeling like I want to be by myself. I have a lot on my mind right now."

"Gabby, tell me what's on your mind, because maybe I can help you."

I had to pause and really get my thoughts together, or else I might have blurted out something at that moment that I regretted.

What came to my mind and what I wanted to say was, "It's about you bitch! Don't play with me and act like you honestly don't have any idea why I'm acting this way towards you. You really can't be serious. Do you understand the words that are coming out of my mouth?"

I couldn't believe the nerve of her. But I stayed silent, because I was so surprised, and her showing up, talking this way, really took me back.

Listen bitch, I kept thinking to myself, what you really want to know is, am I going to tell Rochelle about the affair that you're having with her man?

I took my time answering the stupid question she had just asked me. I said with a fake smile, "No one can help me, and I don't want to burden anyone with my problems."

"Gabby don't be silly. Why don't you come over here, sit next to me on the couch and tell me what's really bothering you?"

I reluctantly got up, walked slowly over to the couch and sat down beside her. Sabrina put her hand on my leg. It startled me and I jumped. She frowned. "Gabby it's only me. So why are you jumping like that? If I didn't know any better, I would think you're scared of me or something. And I don't know why that would be. Hell, I've seen you naked. Why are you treating me like a stranger?"

All I could do was stare at her because I was at a loss for words. I finally decided to tell her.

"Sabrina, are you having an affair with Mike?" I asked in a very soft voice.

She looked surprised that I would even ask her. So she wouldn't give herself away, she started smiling. "No! No! Why would you ask me a question like that?"

"About three or four weeks ago I saw you getting out of his car at your house. And around this time I know for sure that Rochelle was on tour in California. I saw you two kiss and both of you walked in your house together. I thought to myself, 'How could she do that to Rochelle?' I didn't expect that from you especially since we are supposed to be sisters. I mean, you already know the rule—we don't sleep with each other's men."

Sabrina didn't know how to respond to me. She had a look of despair on her face. She looked down and said, "I know that what I've done was very wrong. But it's just something that happened; it wasn't intentionally done to hurt her. I know how I felt when it was done to me. I felt betrayed and hurt. I felt like shit."

Now I'm annoyed. "Well, if you're referring to me, I've already told you several times that I never slept with Philip. I had nothing to do with him breaking up with you. I never had feelings for him, nor did I ever want to get with him. He always tried to get with me, but he's not my type. He tried to push up on me constantly before and after you two got together. And he was told that it was never going to happen between him and me, especially when you two got together. I told him over and over again, that he could always be replaced, but the love and the loyalty that I had for you was forever. You are my sister, and no one or nothing is supposed to come between us, right? Seriously, I would never want to jeopardize our relationship for anything in the world. A true friend is hard to find, but you, on the other hand, crossed that line."

Sabrina leaned toward me. "Well, if our friendship really means that much, and we are truly sisters like you just said, then this one time you won't have a problem keeping this to yourself. It can be our little secret. Do you think that Rochelle tells us everything that she does? I don't think so. I think that there's a lot that we don't know about Miss Benson. Besides, it's going to really hurt her, and she's on the road and doesn't need any distractions."

Sabrina grabbed her purse. "I know that you like money, so I've got something for you." She rummaged inside the purse for a few seconds and then pulled out a wad of money, fifties, twenties and tens. Then she counted it, counting out three hundred dollars, and tried to hand it to me. I frowned because I didn't understand what she was trying to do. I was so taken back that all I could do was shake my head with disbelief.

"Sabrina, why are you giving me this money? I don't need it. I'm good."

Sabrina tried putting the money in my hands. "Take this for yourself." Then she winked at me.

I couldn't believe her. She had really turned into this grimy person that I didn't even know anymore. How could she be that low?

"Are you trying to bribe me with this money that you're giving me? You would actually stoop so low as to offer me this money for my silence?"

"Of course not, silly. I'm just giving you this money so you can get something nice for yourself."

"Sabrina, where did you get this money? Because at the party you claimed that you didn't have any money. And why is there red ink on all the bills? How dare you try to bribe me with your blood money! I'm so insulted right now. I thought that I knew you better than that, but I don't really know what you're capable of. What else have you done that Rochelle, Dom and I don't know about? I know that your closet must be filled with skeletons."

She stared at me, eye to eye. "Listen bitch, don't throw stones, because as I recall, your house is also made of glass. Huh, you are not a goody two-shoes. I don't think that you really want to take that trip down memory lane, do you? Remember, I know quite a few things about you."

"That's beside the point," I answered. "I still don't have to accept this money. I'm still not accepting this money! I don't care what you say. If I take this money, I will be as bad as you, and I want to be able to sleep at night with a clear conscience. Both you and Rochelle are my friends, and I don't want to be put in the middle. I think that you should come clean, and just tell her and get it out in the open. Maybe she will forgive you and maybe she won't. But at least you won't have this hanging over your head."

Sabrina started crying, saying that even if she wanted to tell her, she wouldn't know what to say or how to say it. "You know she's going to go ballistic and I can't afford that. I like the way my face looks. She's not going to take something like this lightly." She dried her eyes and said, "I just can't do it."

She threw the money down on the table. "Gabby, please think about it." Then she jumped up, grabbed her purse and ran to the door like a track star.

Sabrina quickly opened the door, saying before she left, "I hope you'll consider what I said and just keep this between us. I love you, Gabby, and I'll talk to you in a few days."

Then she slammed the door violently behind her, almost knocking all of the pictures off the wall. Sabrina ran to her car, got inside and took off like a bat out of hell. She missed hitting the car in front of her by inches as she disappeared into the night, never once looking back.

TO BE CONTINUED.
SEE HOW THE DRAMA UNFOLDS IN THE SEQUEL!